# Max in America:
## Into the Land of Trump

Also by Henry Chamberlain

*A Night at the Sorrento and Other Stories*

# Henry Chamberlain

# Max in America:
## Into the Land of Trump

*A man without history is a tree without roots.*
  Confucius

**Comics Grinder Productions**
**comicsgrinder.com**

*Faith is taking the first step even when you don't see the whole staircase. Love is the only force capable of transforming an enemy into a friend. Darkness cannot drive out darkness; only light can do that. Hate cannot drive out hate; only love can do that.*

Martin Luther King, Jr.

For Jennifer Daydreamer

# Prologue

It had been a perfect routine for Maximo Viaje: living inside a bubble, as if the perpetual subject of a luxury travel magazine feature. He'd lived the life of a little English prince up until the bottom fell out. At age 55, Maximo had a whole new world to explore and some growing up to do.

He'd been at his mother's side, assisting her with the empire she had built. It had been going on for as long as he could remember and of no big concern to him as long as the good times kept rolling. He'd only known the best in life: doted upon by an eccentric mother who gave him the world as long as he remained in her world. Maximo was a man well-versed in culture with little to no practical knowledge; a man mostly trained in the art of leisure.

Then came the day when he could no longer be a barfly philosopher, a happy-go-lucky Lothario. Suddenly, he was an illegal Mexican immigrant in the United States during a time of heightened intolerance. It came to be known as the Trump era. Now, it felt like he was the perpetual subject of cable news: a scapegoat to be kicked around or a symbol to fetishize.

However, Maximo was indeed a cultured man with a serious creative passion. All along, he'd been pursuing creative projects with all his heart. He always had his art to keep him alive and sane. Perhaps there was an artful way to not only survive but to directly respond to the hatred and intolerance he now found himself experiencing firsthand in the United States of America.

Just looking in the mirror, gave him a road map for what would lay ahead for him. He was a light-skinned man. Despite his beating himself up for being out of touch, he was quite aware of skin tone and the role it could be made to play in society and in messing up people's minds. For some Hispanics, it meant everything to be able to "pass for white." For Maximo, he had the privilege of not being intimidated. He could easily ask: *What's so great about passing for white? What's so great about being white in the first place? Isn't it all just supposed to be a person's complexion? Will we ever be able to honestly accept and warmly welcome any skin tone, any background, and everything else that added up to a human being?*

A whole new way of thinking was emerging, a new generation was waking up, and he could be a part of it. Maybe he'd stumble but he could be a part of it if only people would give him a chance to make mistakes on the way to true enlightenment.

Whatever Maximo did from now on would pale in comparison to his days of leisurely contemplating color theory in regards to his next painting or literary theory in regards to his next novel. It was all suddenly going to get very real for him.

# Max in America:
## Into the Land of Trump

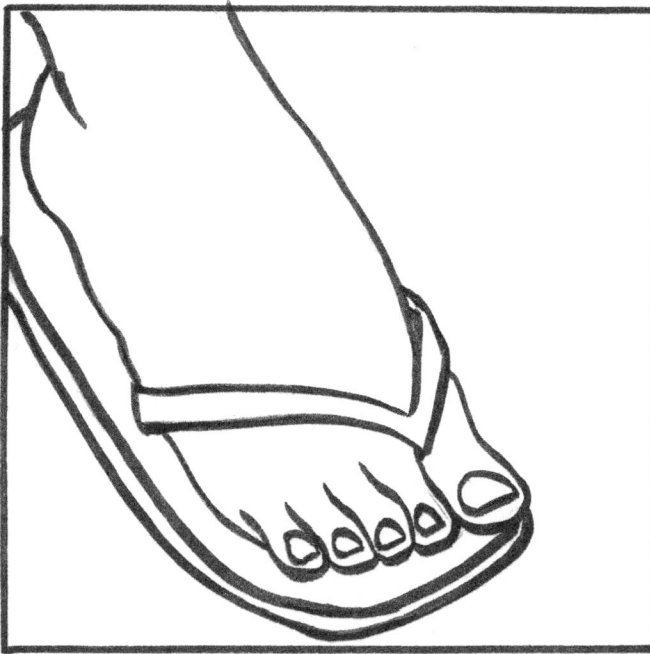

# 1

Mexico City, Summer 2018

Such a delicious night it was, smooth and balmy, caressing his body and relaxing his troubled mind. Little did Maximo know that he'd already begun his journey of a thousand steps that summer night in Mexico City, one that would lead him to the greatest fight of his life. With each new step, he was coming closer and closer to a time of reckoning. It would be a big adventure, more than enough to bring a sparkle to the eyes of any discerning literary agent. It would be his greatest story ever. But, for now, all he had to worry about was his pet dog, Rico. Maybe the little thing had walked enough. Maximo scooped him up and plopped him into his book bag, quite an easy thing to do with a Chihuahua dog. Rico, for his part, was content to fall asleep and be carried around.

It was the night before it happened that Maximo went to get a touch up on his tattoo at Estudio 184, Mexico City's hippest tattoo parlor. He had made his way over to the arts quarter as he did most nights. The colonia of Roma Norte was not far from the highrise he called home. "It's time this got a little bit of a face-lift." Maximo gave a sheepish smile to the tattoo artist who responded with a modest nod. "So, what do you think, Carlos? I think it's just faded out a bit. But, overall, do you like the design?"

It was a common question that Carlos preferred to avoid but he did like the regal lion holding a globe. "I do like it. Where did you find this? What does it mean to you?"

"It's from the house flag of the Cunard cruise line from 1934. I found it in a book at a thrift store and I always thought it would make a great tattoo, you know? It symbolizes, for me, travel and adventure." Maximo gave out a little sigh, "It's there to give me a little boost when I plan my travels and when I'm out there exploring."

"Out where? Do you have some travel plans right now?"

Maximo let himself think for a moment. "Well, you just never know when your next adventure might happen!"

In fact, Maximo was only hours away from a monumental adventure. He had no way of knowing it but he was in for quite a bumpy ride. Maybe a bright light at the end of a tunnel? They say truth is simple and that lies are complex, don't they? Well, it sounds like something that someone would say, someone important imparting great wisdom. It seemed to Maximo that he was always waiting for his great moment, always waiting to be fully heard, fully understood.

Maximo looked like a world traveller, a real jet setter. However, to be honest, Maximo had never ventured anywhere outside his home town of Mexico City. Lucky for him, fate provided him with such a robust international city upon which to strut about. If he allowed himself to dwell upon his true self, he would have to admit that, in many ways, he appeared to be nothing more than one of those sexy

Italian Lotharios, those men who give off a sultry vibe and seem so worldly but are little more than overgrown mama's boys. The lady killer who never moved out of his parent's home and instead opted for a life of unrestricted preening and strutting about. So, yes, there was that side to Maximo but it would be grossly unfair to dismiss him. Maximo was an unapologetic romantic but he was also a serious artist. He worked tirelessly on his creative passions with integrity. At least within local circles, he was regared as an undisputed dedicated artist.

He was there at all the artist gatherings and festivals and gallery receptions. And, from time to time, there he was on stage reciting a poem or in a suit standing in front of one of his paintings for a gallery show. Or, most often, there he was in a café writing the next chapter to his novel. It was all so bohemian. The only problem was that, as the years dragged on, it had become so repetitive. It was time to repair old tattoos. It was time to rethink things. He'd reached a point where he'd begun to really wonder if it was time for a big change.

And then something happened.

# 2

Maximo Viaje lived with his mother on the top floor, the only residence, of the Latin American Tower, that landmark tower that resembles the Empire State Building in the heart of the historic district of Mexico City. Each day, he would accept a modest list of tasks from his mother. By noon, once he was done with his assignments, he would often wander off to the nearby Palacio de Bellas Artes and contemplate the Diego Rivera murals from a catbird seat in the museum café. Some days, when he had no specific errands to run, he might stay home and simply gaze upon that very same cultural center from a sofa, look out the massive floor-to-ceiling windows, and just take in the whole Zocalo scene with its esoteric, aristocratic beauty. No wonder he could easily let himself believe that he was destined for great things with his forever grooming towards something. But his lifestyle was only part of what seemed to set him apart from the average person.

Maximo had been left to feel as if he'd always gotten his way, even if he clearly wasn't. His earliest memories were of coming home with his prized comic books, what looked like bootleg versions of Mickey Mouse and Donald Duck, items his mother was more than happy to buy for him. Looking back, he never noticed any Mexican themed comics, if they existed at all. And his mother never stressed Mexican culture. It had always been more a case of a generic mother and her boy exploring a big and exciting metropolis. Perhaps that is why he never questioned, not until well into adulthood, the lack of diversity in most of the media he consumed from the United States. And, the less he questioned, the better it seemed to be for him overall.

The biggest compromise was that he was never to mention his father: never ask about his father, never bring him up at all. It wasn't an official rule to follow but it was clearly one of those things left mostly unsaid and undeniably enforced.

Then there was that additional touch of strange that completely tipped the balance: Maximo was born a half hour past noon on November 22, 1963. How was that possible? How could it be that he was born on such an infamous date: the precise time of the assassination of President Kennedy? As a child, when he was just old enough to acknowledge world events, he thought this was witchcraft. At around the age of 8, Maximo suspected his mother of being a witch and of conjuring him up at precisely that unholy hour.

Of course, as Maximo grew older, he resigned himself to his diabolical birthday. He matured and, in order to survive, he wised up to the basic facts of life: you can be as eccentric as you please but leave room for conventional reality, the accepted status quo. And so, knowing in his heart that he was a creative oddball of strange origin, he succumbed to a routine that seemed to suit his clandestine destiny. And, at every opportunity, his mother suggested, advised, and conjured his fate in a desired direction. Within a decade of his first suspecting his mother of being a witch, he had become her apprentice. He became an assistant to his mother and her mysterious real estate empire to which he was given limited access. He really had no idea how big or how small it was but it was undoubtedly big enough. Day to day menial tasks kept him busy: making bank deposits, sorting through mail, whatever. He asked no questions lest he end up picking up more cumbersome responsibilities. He did what he was told. And then he went off to play as he saw fit: wine, women, and song for life!

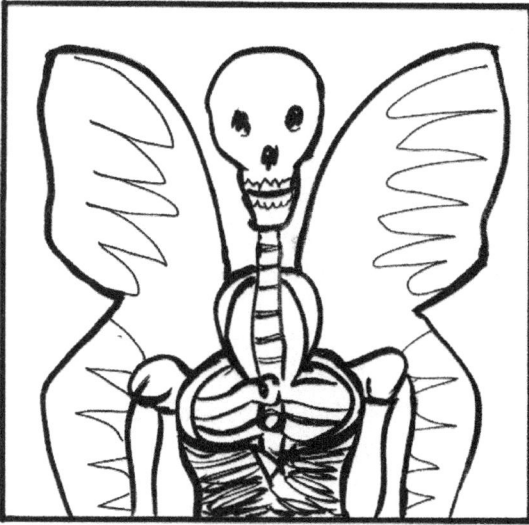

# 3

Maximo's true destiny was not to unfold significantly for many years to come. In fact, Maximo had begun to lose any hope that his youthful aspirations would ever fully blossom as he had dreamt they would. Like many an emerging artist, he had seen his work appear in various places but, in his view, it was of no lasting value. He had not made his mark and, by the age of fifty, he was ready to accept his fate as a happy-go-lucky amateur. He never reached that level of excellence he had sought. Maybe he hadn't been looking in the right places. But all would most definitely change for him and in a most abrupt way. At the start of what seemed to be just a very typical day, with nothing special on the agenda, Maximo found his mother dead in her office. She looked frozen and had apparently died during the night.

The shock of his mother's death was so big that it left Maximo utterly speechless. He had walked down the long corridor to her office and found her slumped down on her chair, surrounded by assorted documents, an adding machine stuck in time as her hand lay on the keys causing it to perpetually sputter out calculations no longer based upon any reality having to do with properties, commercial, residential, or otherwise. There was no pulse. No doubt, she was dead.

Rico let out a long sustained howl and this was the sound that kept Maximo alert and able to make the long walk back to the living room, pumped up with just enough presence of mind to call the police. He was able to speak clearly and was assured an ambulance was on its way. He had performed what was to be his last task in the service of The Viaje Organization. He gently returned the old-fashioned phone to its cradle. And he then promptly fainted, falling backward onto the floor. Rico licked his face and finally succumbed to slumber nestled in the crook of Maximo's neck.

Within an hour, Maximo's position was no longer so stable and to be taken for granted. They arrived in freshly pressed suits, stinking of arrogant cologne, and looking none too friendly. This was still Maximo's home, or so he told himself, the only home he had ever known. But not so much--not when the matriarch was now dead. Suddenly, he was not someone to be indulged, to be tolerated, to be accepted as a permanent fixture. For fixture he no longer was. Suddenly, he was a man with no history, no country, no anything!

# 4

"I'm not welcome here anymore?" asked Maximo, his eyes closed so as not to address anyone in particular.

Someone chuckled. It was a friendly chuckle, not necessarily meant to offend.

"Where am I supposed to live? What am I supposed to do now?" pleaded Maximo.

One of the members of the team finally drew closer. This man had no distinguishing features, nothing that set him apart from this team or any other team. But he was relatively handsome and seemed capable. "Mr. Viaje, there is a problem," said this nondescript but amicable man. He looked down to the floor. "It seems that the world has grown around you as it did your mother. We appreciate what your mother did as a building manager but this quaint arrangement has come to an end."

"What do you mean? You worked for her, right? You are part of The Viaje Organization. Does that not mean anything in regards to me?" It was a question that hung in the air.

"I'm very sorry, sir. But we can't sustain this arrangement any longer. Your mother's position, well, she outlived it. We don't need a replacement for this specific assignment. Therefore, the compensation of living quarters must come to an end. I'm very sorry but that means that you will have to find somewhere else to live."

Maximo, in his fractured state of mind, was still able to concede that he had been living under a delusion. His mother never ran an empire of any kind. Her connection to this corporation was like that of a tick to a dog. He would have to abide by what these gentlemen were there to achieve. He wanted to go peacefully, without incident and his dignity still intact. He struggled to hide his despair.

"Of course, you can stay the night, sir. Get your affairs in order as best you can."

"I don't know exactly where to begin but perhaps a good meal, a day to think, and a night's sleep will help me find my way. But what about my mother? And what about all the details that follow? Oh, my head is swimming!"

The faceless but capable man tried to pat Maximo's back but then held back. "True, there are potentially unresolved little details but surely, sir, they are simply small matters. And that may take some time to sort out. What we must do now is to set boundaries and that means, sadly, your departure. Your mother's funeral is something we are prepared for. She chose her cemetery plot years ago. You may know that. She also reserved a plot for you, next to her, when the time comes."

Hearing this only irritated Maximo. "My mother went to the trouble of arranging my own funeral but not my future. A man must live before he dies!"

"There seems to be little else to say for now, sir. Our deepest apologies go out to you. Unfortunately, we never got to know each other. You made no effort to network with us. You were a dark phantom. And perhaps therein lies part of your problem."

"Oh, I don't need to be lectured!" Maximo motioned them to the door. "Please, I will use my time wisely. When I'm done, I will leave the key on the counter and close the door on my way out."

"That is agreeable, sir." Everyone walked out at a respectful pace with their heads hanging down as far as they could go.

Maximo watched them, as they heavily leaned downward and out of his sight. In direct response, Maximo straightened himself up and held his head up high. In so doing, it gave him an idea and a means of escape from his current predicament.

# 5

Maximo had paid some attention to the latest promotional campaign to entice new rentals. It revolved around the theme of lifting up one's spirit. And the centerpiece was a hot air balloon. It was a nice and plump old-fashioned thing decked out with colorful festoons and a banner proclaiming the beauty of flight. It was Maximo's time to fly away from the nest.

Maximo took the elevator up to the top floor and then climbed some steps leading him to the rooftop. He was only wearing some casual beach wear, shorts, t-shirt, and flip flops, but had made sure to pack a light bag with a few essentials, including Rico. And there it was, a hot air balloon worthy of Phileas Fogg! But Maximo wouldn't need to go around the world. He would just need to make it across only one border. That wasn't asking too much, was it? And crossing that border would have serious consequences. But he wasn't thinking about the U.S. border patrol. No, he was most concerned with what might happen if he finally met his father. That had never even been a possibility before this moment!

It was quite obvious to him that there was a strong likelihood that his father was Anglo. He'd even go as far as to suggest there was something to be said for his father being a Kennedy! Maximo had a Boston Brahmin patrician quality about him, a certain New England reserve, that kept him aloof and out of place no matter how hard he tried. When he thought he was relaxed and happy, to others he looked as if he was frowning. He didn't particularly care about it but, all the same, he enjoyed having this weird sense of style and dry demeanor. He and his mother binged on shows from the BBC. Truth be told, he lived mostly in his head and his head told him he was best suited for life in a post-war London flat. And there was one more thing. He had to admit that, at his core, there was something very Kennedyesque about him. He'd observed, with a bit of disgust, how American politicians attempted to channel JFK with the hairstyle or with a few documents tucked into a side pocket of a suit jacket. For Maximo, whatever this Kennedy connection was, the sad distant eyes or the bookish detachment, it came natural to him.

Without giving it any further consideration, Maximo set off on the next phase of his life. He undid straps, readjusted lines, let out gears, and off he went before he had another moment to back out of it. Within just a few minutes, he was airborne. The contraption just kept lifting further and further up. It was a lazy Sunday morning and that, no doubt, was to Maximo's advantage. There would be no stopping him. No one would think to look for him in the first place. No one would notice his escape.

I'm a desperate soul, Maximo mused to himself. Why else would I be attempting to flee in this bloated pleasure craft?

Bloated or not, the hot air balloon proved to be a persistent beast. It just kept going and going, pushing past its own purpose and limitations. This was one determined balloon!

"Mother? Are you there?" pleaded Maximo.

# 6

Hot air balloons are supposed to be fairly predictable—but not this one.

"Balloons do what they will do," sighed Maximo, "This one is actually going to take me to where I want to go!"

Maximo had been carefully following the terrain down below. All he could see were mountains. "Mama, you're such a good pilot! You're following along the spine of the mighty mountains!"

It had been a quiet ride for a very long time until gusts of wind helped to pick up the pace. "I study these cloud formations and I see a church sitting high above and just behind it, the moon! The sky is half light and half shadow!"

"I am half light and half shadow."

The winds kept coming and rocked Maximo's hearty ship. "We're moving a little bit faster!" Maximo held on tight. "I wish that, whatever happens next, I continue to move forward. I never wished to be the fool. Perhaps I will come into full bloom in this next chapter of my life."

# 7

High winds soon gave way to intense heat. Maximo was sweating like mad. He was literally dripping wet. "Oh, God, Rico, you're trembling. This heat will kill us both!" Maximo took off his shirt and covered Rico with it. Maximo hid directly under the balloon for shade. "I will maintain this shaded pose for as long as we need to!" He was literally in a fetal position. "I will remain coiled up, as in the womb, waiting to be reborn!"

Maximo lost track of time and fell into a deep sleep. A sudden jolt woke him up and he stood up to review his progress. "Wait, I can clearly see the Baja peninsula!" As if by a miracle, the balloon was making a swift dash over the border. "I have no doubt that I've just crossed into the United States of America!" And, with that cheerful comment, fate stepped in again. The heat finally ate away at the balloon and caused it to dip, to swoon, and start to crumble. It was coming down fast!

"Oh, no!" Maximo was beyond frightened. All he could do was hold on tight for a crash landing. Everything was tumbling back and forth. "I can't die like this!"

Rico was wide awake and barked his little heart out. He tried to jump in order to look out.

The balloon landed in the water, not far from shore. It gave Maximo a safe landing after all. "I must swim like I've never swum before! This is the ocean! There could be sharks!" Maximo was not a very good swimmer but he dog-paddled like crazy. Of course, Rico, being a dog, was much better as dog-paddling and quickly surpassed his master. After some frantic swimming, Maximo tried to stand up and he discovered he was standing in shallow waters! He'd already made it to land! He walked up the beach. He was alone with himself and the beach. And he loved it.

But you're never too far from something even if you're walking toward nothing. Not too far off in the distance, he noticed someone. He was about to call out when he realized his throat was dry and raspy. He would need to get closer. Apparently, Rico had beat him and was getting acquainted with a lovely young woman.

# 8

As far as anyone was concerned, it was just another casual day on a beach in La Jolla. It must have still been early morning of the following day. He'd completely lost track of time. There was not another soul except for Maximo and Rico and their new friend. If anyone had even bothered to look up in the sky, maybe the crash landing would have looked more like some kooky freefalling drone. Maximo walked up and the woman didn't look concerned at all and remained very calm as he approached. There seemed to be a hint of a smile, something inviting about her.

Maximo took in the woman's kind face. He lingered over her enigmatic smile. He hoped that her smile, her whole person, was warming up to him.

"I see you've met Rico."

"He's cute."

"I wonder if you can help me? My name is Maximo."

The woman looked intrigued. "Help you with what?"

"I've been in an accident."

"Oh, my. I'm sorry. What happened?"
"It's a complicated thing. I just fell out of the sky."

The woman laughed. "You what?"

Maximo, feeling helpless, kept his composure. "I know this sounds unusual. But I was in a hot air balloon." He turned around and scanned the shore. He had to admit that he was disoriented so he tried to simply remain calm. "Out there. I don't see it anymore but I was in a hot air balloon and it crashed."

The woman looked out in the direction he was pointing at, couldn't see signs of a wreckage, but instantly believed him. "I hope you're alright. You look like you're fine. Just look at you, a very healthy man, I should say." Maximo wondered why she would have felt compelled to say he looked healthy but tried to ignore it. He needed to hold steady and not have her regret talking to him in the first place.

"My name is Maximo. I would be grateful to you if you could help me."

"Maximo, huh? I like that name! Sounds very regal," said the woman with some gusto. Maximo shifted his weight, becoming a bit more self-conscious, but mostly exhausted and bewildered.

"I'm Leslie. I will help you on one condition."

"Yes, what is the condition?"

"Rico must join us!"

"Done!"

They quietly walked together. Maximo was like an explorer being guided by a friendly native back to her hut or to her castle, he had no idea which. Rico did not sound off any alarms, and instead wildly wagged his tail. So, here was a human being helping out another human being who was going to complicate her life in all sorts of ways. Maximo was in awe of all of this goodwill. He needed to understand what was motivating this altruism but the fact remained that he rarely, if ever, connected with someone who truly tickled his senses in the way that Leslie was doing.

# 9

When Maximo and Leslie made it back to her hotel room, they did not miss a beat and allowed themselves a kiss—and an embrace. It happened so fast and it had been so smooth. It surprised him. Was this a welcoming kiss and hug? Then she stepped back and looked him over and this gave Maximo a chance to study her in the cozy indoor light. Maybe she was working something out in her mind, in her life. Maximo could sense he was already letting go or, at least, not impatiently holding on. Maybe she was testing him out. But, the more he pondered over this, the more his journey came back to him and started to pull him down. Was she going through something right now too? He found himself raising his hands up a little, like a professor about to start a lecture or to show just how clueless he really was.

"Let me say a few things."

"You really want to ruin the moment?"

"No."

"Then don't say anything."

He took those words to heart and remained silent. She bent down to pat Rico on his head. "Let me see what we can do for your dog." Leslie looked over her options. "Will he be okay with some cereal and milk?"

"Rico will eat just about anything."

"Except chocolate, right? Aren't dogs supposed to explode if they eat chocolate?"

"I think Rico could handle it but let's not try it out."

Leslie dropped a blanket and some pillows in a corner of the kitchen and Rico collapsed in the snug spot she'd created for him.

"That's better. Go on, please. I know you wanted to say something."

At that very moment, Maximo would have been content with Leslie simply throwing a pillow and blanket out for him to collapse upon but he forged on. "Like I started to say, I have had a very complicated accident. I'm just catching my breath over what's happened on the most eventful day or so of my life so far!"

"Oh, really? Where do I fit into this?"

"You fit in very well."

"Do tell."

"Well, let me start back to what triggered all this. You see, my mother passed away."

"I'm so sorry to hear that, Maximo."

Maximo looked off into the distance. "I found her dead Sunday morning. I'd been out and she probably passed away sometime during the night. Arrangements were made within the hour. And that set all sorts of things into motion, more than I have had a chance to process."

"Where does the hot air balloon adventure come in?"

"I hopped into that balloon and it ultimately crash landed here."

"But how did that happen? Really, a hot air balloon?"

"Oh, it was part of a promotion back at the office. I helped myself to it."

"Is this near La Jolla?"

"No, no. This was in Mexico City."

"Mexico City?"

"I know. It's pretty wild."

"It's more than that. It's somehow…magical."

"Magical. Yes, perhaps supernatural."

"And you're Mexican, right?"

"Yes, I am Maximo from Mexico."

"Oh, my, when I wait for just the right guy, I hit the jackpot!

# 10

Maximo and Leslie were curled up in bed. They must have been too exhausted to do more than fall asleep. They both needed naps. And those naps lasted throughout the night. As a new day arrived, Maximo awoke to a completely new life. And it seemed like a very nice one. He was wearing silk pajamas that felt like heaven. Leslie had on a matching pair. That was sort of weird but also so incredibly comfortable.

"You are a kind soul," he whispered in her ear. He rested his hand on her hip and nuzzled up close.

"It takes one to know one," she whispered back.

He put his arm around her waist and she suddenly jerked back. "What is that?" Maximo was confronted by a large blue butterfly, all shiny and full of fluttery vigor.

"This Morpho butterfly is a symbol of good luck in Mexico! We also have the Monarch butterflies that bathe everyone with goodwill. Ah, but the Morpho, they are very special. They will bring us good luck!" Maximo snatched it up and jumped out of bed. He opened the patio door and walked out onto the deck. "Fly away my little blue friend. You're free!"

Leslie sat up in bed. She had a serious look. "We need to talk."

Already it's time for the talk? Maximo couldn't help but lose his good humor. Like a dog that had misbehaved, he was suddenly self-conscious, tensing up as if walking with his tail between his legs. Rico noticed and let out with a long but muted howl, apropos for the moment.

"I want to let you know," said Leslie, looking every bit alert and earnest, "there's nothing at all that you can tell me that I'm not open to hearing, okay? Life can be crazy. I have my own crazy stuff. I am talking cra-cra. Really out there. Maybe we will have good luck. But maybe it'll be crazy good luck. Is that good? I don't know!"

"That sounds okay by me." He needed to listen and understand what was upsetting Leslie so much. This might be it, the big moment that explained the strange kiss and the silk pajamas.

"You look exactly like my fiancée. Or, should I say, ex-fiancée. I can tell certain things that are different. You wear your hair a little different. You have a little more weight on you. But most people would never know the difference. Well, except for one distinct difference," she motioned to his arms with tattoos. "But, aside you're your tattoos, you guys look totally alike. You really do. You look that much like him!" Her voiced rose as she spoke, as if just freed from a great burden. She looked like she was about to cry.

Maximo slumped down at the foot of the bed and massaged Leslie's feet. His head was spinning. This made no sense at all unless it was as crazy as he thought it could be but it couldn't be that. Could it?

"I don't know. He could be your twin! Seriously, you both look that much alike."

"A twin." The word triggered him into a tailspin. Maximo froze. He felt a cool bead of sweat roll down his back. That could explain many things.

"When was he born?"

"Well, you won't believe this. He was born on November 22, 1963. You know…"

Maximo's back stiffened. "Yes, I do know."

"The worst part, I think, is the name they gave him. John F. Kennedy."

"My God!"

"He avoids it as much as he can. People just call him 'John' and that sounds normal."

Maximo shook his head. There is nothing normal about this! Is this my destiny? Was I destined to seduce the woman who was involved with my long lost twin? No, my journey goes much further, it goes back to my father! "Listen, Leslie, tell me where John was born."

Leslie hesitated as she sensed a major unraveling. "Mexico City."

Maximo let his head gently fall at Leslie's feet. She lifted one foot and smoothed her toes across his forehead as if combing his hair.

"Mexico City. I believe we have a match."

# 11

It was on the way back to Seattle that Maximo became more familiar with what to expect in the near future. He surprised himself by agreeing so quickly to assume the identity of his phantom twin. There was no other way. Leslie had done an excellent job of explaining the situation to him. She and John had come down for a romantic getaway. They'd never been to La Jolla. They were there to visit John's parents, no big deal. Then they had this fight. It wasn't typical bickering either. This one was big enough to be a breaking point. Looking back on it now, Leslie concluded it all came down to the simple fact that John was an asshole. He could be nice. He could even be warm. But it always came back to him being an alpha dog asshole. In a sense, he couldn't help it. That's how he was built. Anyway, he marched out and decided to go visit his parents on his own and leave her to figure out how to get back home. In his haste, he left everything behind, including his wallet. He'd had these sort of tantrums before and maybe this one required him to learn his lesson. So, why not have Maximo take over for a while—maybe even for good?

"It was so easy to go through airport security. Do they ever look closely and carefully compare people with their identification?" Maximo was expecting the worst considering the near panic mode in Trump's America he was so used to seeing on cable news. Leslie could only shrug. They were together, a cozy couple flying first class after a whirlwind romantic vacation. Everything was perfectly normal except she returned with a completely different man.

Leslie had made sure to buy Maximo a backpack and loaded it up with tourist junk so that he would look less conspicuous to TSA. Once they arrived at Sea-Tac, they quickly went through baggage claim and then made it out to the parking lot. She tossed his bag into her trunk along with her own luggage. She took the driver's seat and welcomed her new passenger. As if in a dream, the two seemed to be floating along. Leslie usually hated the long drive home from the airport but not this time. "Look, there it is," she said as the city came into view. "Some people like to call it the Emerald City."

Maximo had never given much thought to Seattle, although he was aware of how it had grown in prominence over the years. "Ah, it is a pretty city."

Leslie could only laugh. "It's pretty but it's become a little ugly too like an exotic flower that's been over-cultivated to where a vital force has been sucked out of it."

Maximo turned abruptly to see if Leslie was serious. She was. "Well, cities are delicate organisms, that's for sure."

Leslie shrugged again. "Tell that to the developers or to the city council! Seattle has steadily become overcrowded with no plan in place other than wishful thinking from the hard left. No one is to be arrested unless perhaps they murder someone. I'm tired of having to watch my step for heroin needles and not feeling safe. Look, I'm liberal but I'm no fan of extremism, whether right or left."

The sedan pulled into a driveway in an immaculately kept neighborhood. It was midday. Maximo was pleased to take in all the lush greenery. "Everyone has a garden it seems."

Leslie nodded. "Yeah, people take their egos all the way to the property line. More vegetation than one could ever eat. More flowers and trees to ensure a high pollen count. Don't get me wrong: it does look oh so nice. And it's summer, the best time of year in Seattle."

"Seattle. In my wildest dreams, I never saw myself this far north."

"You are in a special kind of place. It's, how should I say this, a mix of old and new. The old is giving way to the new. The more conservative working class are being pushed out by the more liberal and younger tech crowd."

"It all sounds quite fascinating."

"I do love it here. But I grew up here and I have a very long memory. I remember when it used to be more quiet and sensible. Anyway, I want you to enjoy it. We're close enough to five or six coffee shops. You can't enjoy Seattle without a cup of coffee."

"It won't be anything new for me, Leslie," snapped back Maximo. "I mean, we have numerous coffee shops in Mexico City. It's a major urban center in the world, you know. I've lived a very cosmopolitan life. I'm a writer and an artist. I have numerous manuscripts and a studio full of paintings back home…"

"Whoa, there, I believe you. You're singing to the choir with me!" Leslie gave him a hug to try to reassure him.

After a quick unpacking, Leslie escorted Maximo to the nearest coffee shop. It was a quaint local coffee roaster located in a repurposed Victorian house. An older man, apparently a customer just leaving, wearing a crisp print shirt and natty baseball cap, nodded knowingly at Maximo. "Hola, amigo!" It was such an odd and random gesture. Was Maximo supposed to be offended or was he supposed to take it in stride? Maximo looked at Leslie for help. "Don't get me started," she said and just shook her head.

They settled down in a cozy spot in the café, each with a big mug of coffee. Maximo asked, "What did you mean by that? Is there a lot of racism here?"

Leslie gave a wry smile. "You wouldn't think it. But it's here. There's a lot of a certain kind here that is very passive-aggressive. You could almost miss it if you weren't the target of it. I know exactly what I'm talking about. I'm the girl who was dating your twin. I'll notice it, even if John doesn't. I can tell you a lot about what you'll experience here based on that." Maximo let that sink in. Now, in this new environment, it felt like his Hispanic features dominated over his Anglo features, no matter how evenly split his genetic makeup.

Maximo thought over where he was. "I can't help but think there are a lot of people here attempting to do the right thing."

Leslie nodded. "A lot of them are trying way too hard, like you're a special project. But there's good news. Seattle is a sanctuary city, after all. That could come in handy for you."

"And it's so serene and mellow here."

"Exactly. A neurotic and chilly sort of mellow"

"A lot of well-intentioned liberals, right?"

"Yes, but just because seemingly well-intentioned liberals appear to want to help you doesn't mean they consider you an equal. A lot of them are as racist, maybe even more so, than anyone else. But I digress."

"Very messed up. Cra-cra messed up."

"Yeah, things are messed up just enough where you can't feel totally good about yourself. They can make sure to leave a lingering doubt. Like a jolly, 'Hola, amigo,' coming randomly out of someone's ass. Your Otherness becomes you. You amuse them. You give them the theme for their next coffee klatch at the local community center. They'll discuss how you can help them shed their white burden."

"Maybe I can help them shed their white burden. All I want to do is help."

"The thing you need to know about Seattle is that it has had big city dreams right from the start—and not just any big city but a special ideal big city. But it hasn't figured out how to deal with big city realities. Homelessness. Crime. Violence. Drugs. A big city can't afford to turn these issues into abstractions and just experiment with them. I shouldn't say too much more right now. I'm tired. But look at it this way: the yellow brick road has brought you to the Emerald City but you'll find the same letdown once you pull back the curtain. Those in charge think they know better than anyone else but they're really just making it up as they go along."

# 12

Maximo woke up the next day in the mood to be creative and proactive. "Leslie, I want to confront this passive-aggressive weird animosity that lurks around here and, I assume, across this country in different ways."

Leslie appreciated the enthusiasm. She laughed, "Yes, in very different ways! Some people don't beat around the bush and would just as soon beat your brains in!"

"Beat my brains in? Just for showing I've got some brains?"

"All the more reason."

Leslie looked over Maximo and gently ran her fingers through her hair. "Here we have a very interesting scenario. A tall good-looking, erudite and sexy, might I add, Mexican man lost in America and speaking out. I'm sure you can do something for the cause!"

"Where to begin, Leslie?"

"I think you could get up on stage and just be yourself."

"On stage? You mean do performance art?"

"Whatever works. Seattle has plenty of places for a passionate person like yourself to reach out to the public. You could do spoken word or maybe even a comedy act. There's a bit of everything, lots and lots of performing arts. As a humble member of the audience, I sometimes don't know whether I'm supposed to look serious or laugh out loud."

"Oh, I would make myself clear. I wouldn't be wasting anyone's time."

"I'm sure you wouldn't."

"Yes, I can reach people with just the right mix of drama and humor. Every bit can help in these crazy and dark times we're living in."

Leslie tried to busy herself by preparing breakfast for them. It was surreal how the time was passing by and she had slipped into a new routine with a new man. She looked at him. He was pacing around. Just like her own John would sometimes do. Could it be this Kennedy thing they seemed to share? Her John had never spoken about it. No doubt, something was going on. Just to look at him, Maximo clearly had that same patrician flair, that Kennedy slow-burn fire in the belly. When the stars were in alignment, no one conveyed that sense of urgency better than a Kennedy. Maximo was, without pretense, tapping into that energy.

"You are going to make a difference, Maximo."

"I feel it in my bones."

Leslie almost cried.

# 13

Back at the home office, Maximo's whereabouts had been duly noted. It turned out that the hot air balloon had a GPS tracking device. Not only that, Maximo asked Leslie if he could use her phone to check in on things back in Mexico City. He had nothing to hide. It was just a matter of time when he got a call back and it happened soon enough. Leslie's phone rang. She took the call. A man with a pleasant yet nondescript voice explained who he was. Leslie said she'd get Maximo for him.

"Hello," Maximo answered.

"Greetings, sir. I do not mean to startle you. I'm just returning your call. In fact, we're happy that you've taken the initiative to venture off as you did. Of course, you can keep the hot air balloon with our compliments."

"It's been destroyed. It tore up on the way here. But thank you all the same."

"Again, we wish you well. And we're still sifting through matters pertaining to any claims you may have. In that spirit, one of our staff happened upon some material that you will find of interest. Apparently, you mother did not rid herself of every trace of your father. We have a journal of his! We think it's something you'd like to look at now. Perhaps it may provide some comfort...and some answers."

"I'm really thrilled to hear this! Yes, by all means, please do send this to me."

"Where should we mail it?"

"I don't know. I don't know. I'll have to ask and get that address to you. I most certainly welcome this treasure. I do want to see it as soon as possible. Would you send it through FedEx?"

"Yes, of course!"

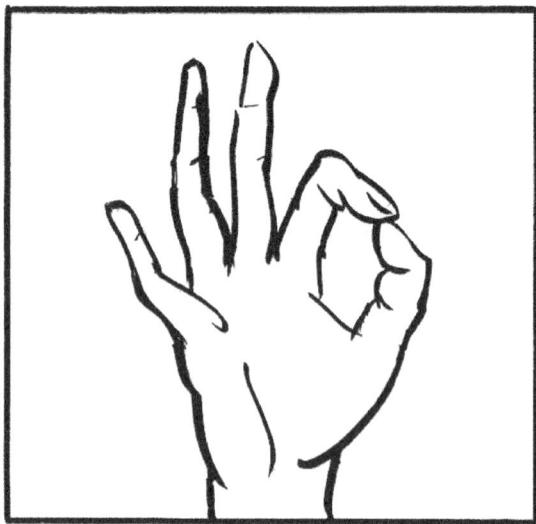

# 14

The package arrived the very next day as promised. Maximo signed for it and immediately tore open the wrapping.

It was a leather bound book that began to crackle at even the slightest opening, as if attempting to whisper its secrets. The brown leather had aged to a fine patina, easily fifty years-old or more. Maximo let his hand glide past page after page, each slightly worn and yellowed, many apparently stuck together. It was a bit of a hodgepodge of carefully laid out notes, lists, assorted ephemera, even sketches, much of it written with relatively fine penmanship, likely with a fountain pen. All these writings and scrawlings, reaching beyond the decades, seemed to be begging to be given their due. A fair amount were sayings, or quotes, in rather plain English. Was it a code? It began with a bit of instruction in the way of an introduction:

*"When you engage in conversation, be sure to establish the focus on the person you are conversing with. This is all about that person.*

*Use that person's name as there is nothing more pleasant to someone than the sound of their own name."*

It was a simple observation. Did it mean anything more? That was all there was on that first page.

Maximo turned that page to consider another of these passages quite suitable for a fortune cookie:

*"When life hands you lemons, make lemonade."*

Leslie had stepped out to do some errands and left Maximo to his own devices. She knew he would be contending with this mysterious book. He meditated upon some of the key quotes and then reread them again and again. Americana at its best: easy to digest and regurgitate. For all he knew, it could be code for something else, hiding in plain sight, masquerading as earnest homespun sayings:

*"Any fool can criticize, condemn, and complain but it takes character and self-control to be understanding and forgiving."*

Was this text part of some campaign? Maximo thought back to all he knew about the USA. It was a country of great eloquence as well as horrid cliché. The contents of this book struck him as assembling that which would appeal to an average audience that relied upon comforting Americana. The message was direct and easy to digest. What current slogan came to mind? Oh, right: *Make. America. Great. Again.* Was his father trying to tell him something about the future?

# 15

When Leslie returned, she opened the front door to find Maximo absorbed in reciting lines from a page. He had the full length mirror out in the living room and it looked like he was rehearsing. "Leslie! I've figured out something! I have put together a little act that will satisfy a number of needs. It will allow me to connect with my new community. It will allow me to speak out. And, I believe, it will allow me to better understand the phantom that is my own father!"

Leslie rushed over to hug Maximo. "Oh, honey, I leave you alone for just a few hours and you have this major catharsis! What to do with you?" She caressed his face and kissed him.

"Let me try to do this in front of you. Ah, my first audience—of one!"

Maximo lowered his head for a moment to concentrate. He imagined himself walking out from behind a curtain and taking the stage to supportive applause.

"Hello. I am Maximo from Mexico. I have crossed over into the United States in an illegal hot air balloon. I think I'll be okay. At least, I'm not in a cage. I'm okay and I'm not in a cage. Sounds good to me so far!"

Leslie immediately laughed. She started to clap thinking that was the end of it but Maximo continued.

"*Make America Great Again*. Is that a joke? Or is it code? It was something that Ronald Reagan used in his campaign for president. Was it only a joke back then? Or was it code back then too? Maybe it began as a simple enough slogan, I think. But today is seems to mean everything and nothing all at the same time. It is a rallying cry for something. It is a way to strike fear.

"I ask you, friends, to be kind and to be good to yourselves. All that kindness and goodness should then easily roll over from you to me and back again," Maximo then held for a beat before proceeding. "How do you like to be treated? Do you appreciate being treated with respect? Or do you prefer to be approached with a touch of a condescending tone? I'm just wondering if someone instantly speaking to me in Spanish is really the way to go. I'll tell you something, I prefer English. My Spanish is okay but I'm not someone to practice your Spanish on."

Leslie was laughing uncontrollably. "Oh, baby, I know what you're saying!"

"Well, it's an interesting time to say the least. Your Trump is quite a handful. If he somehow became the president of Mexico, people would be outraged to the point that everything would be in chaos. Maybe you are a little more understanding. Or maybe the chaos coming from Trump is so bad that it has left you numb. Well, don't be numb! Never be numb. Or as Winston Churchill, once simply regarded as a great leader during World War II and now being called out as a bit of a white supremacist, once said in a genuine moment of inspiring resolve: '*Never Surrender!*'"

Leslie applauded wildly. *"Never Surrender!"*

"Believe in yourself! I believe in you!"

Leslie was in awe. Maximo took a bow. She rushed over to hug him. "You're my hero!" She kissed him full on the mouth and they ran back to her bedroom.

# 16

Time was ticking away. Maximo and Leslie rushed to find any open mic opportunity they could seize upon. "Look, you can perform at a comedy club tonight if you think you're ready!" Maximo stared at Leslie. "I can't afford to get more prepared than I already am. I can do it. I need to feel what it's like."

The two went downtown and signed up on the list for open mic. They had arrived early and managed to snag a spot. Maximo had gotten self-conscious at the last minute and asked Leslie if he should wear a suit. That was no problem at all. John was a financial adviser and practically lived in suits. So, Maximo arrived for his first ever comedy gig in the U.S. as the best dressed performer of the night.

It had been such a hot summer. The edge had finally come off as August gave way to September. It was the Labor Day weekend. That fall would see Trump facing off his first midterm election. Here was Maximo right in the thick of it with something to say.

"I thought I'd wear a suit tonight, folks. A nice suit, any suit, commands some respect. Or maybe it makes me look more like a head waiter. Even that is okay by me. I guess I just wanted to feel good about myself. I'm Mexican and, according to your president, Mexicans are not to be trusted, not to be embraced, not even to be treated as human beings. That's enough to make anyone put on a suit and hide behind whatever respectability it can give. You don't think of Mexicans crossing illegally into the U.S. in suits. No, you think of a Mexican in a suit and you might lose your frame of reference. Who is he? Is he an insurance agent? Or maybe he's a comedian? You just don't know. Well, in a suit or not, even naked, I hope to keep you guessing and thinking. We're all just people, full of hopes and dreams…and sexual fantasies—but I digress. What matters most is being human and embracing humanity."

The audience applauded that night and kept on applauding. Maximo had touched a nerve. He had challenged people to not get too comfortable.

All had gone well. It seemed like nothing could go wrong until Maximo walked off stage and met up with Leslie. She gave an awkward shrug and her smile seemed more of a plea for help. "We need to leave now, Maximo. I mean, now!"

# 17

"Don't worry about paying me or anything like that. You two need to get settled in and follow your dreams."

He doesn't care if he gets paid and he wants people to follow their dreams? Who talks like that? Jimmy Gold is who. He can afford it. He's got the heart and the bank account. Jimmy was Leslie's manager when she was in show business. It seemed like ages ago but now was the time to dust off old dreams.

The night that Maximo had his successful gig in Seattle was the night that Leslie found out that John was on his way back. He'd arrive later that week. The only solution that made sense was for Maximo and Leslie to head out of Seattle and head over to Hollywood. They packed the Subaru with a bunch of essentials, found proper dog food for Rico, and off they went.

Leslie drove all day. She told Maximo about her own dreams of doing standup comedy and how she met John, moved to Seattle, and put her plans on hold. It clicked in her mind that, with Maximo, she could set herself back on track. She knew how to put jokes together and how to engage an audience. She knew how to create characters and how to work with other comedians. And she knew Jimmy Gold.

Actually, it had been only a couple of years, a blink of an eye, since Leslie Mane had seen Jimmy Gold. Just before she left for Seattle, Jimmy had told her that she was always welcome back and to look him up if she should ever need anything. Jimmy meant it. He believed in Leslie. Now, she was back and with Maximo. The three of them met up at Musso & Frank Grill, the legendary Hollywood restaurant. They sat at the Charlie Chaplin booth, the first booth and the only one near a window. This was Chaplin's favorite spot for small groups. There was another booth he liked for larger groups in the main dining room. The whole place looked as if time had stood still long enough to pick up layer upon layer of extraordinary moments, the power and energy of so many talented and powerful spirits.

Jimmy signaled the waiter over, a dapper old fellow in a traditional red and black uniform. "Hey, Lou, I brought a bottle of my own. Couldn't help bringing over the good stuff. Chateau Lafite Rothschild, 2014."

"That is an excellent year for a Bordeaux, sir," said Lou, with a natural deference. He gently picked up the bottle, held it up for Jimmy to examine, and proceeded to uncork it and serve.

Jimmy beamed at his guests during the whole ritual. "I want you guys to relax. I hear from Leslie that you've been on a very long non-stop drive. You're going to need a place to stay so just stay at that little rental of mine on Venice Beach. That will be the perfect place for you two."

Leslie reached over and squeezed Jimmy's hand. "I can't tell you how much that means to me. We'll pay you when we can."

"Seriously, Leslie, the place is not in use right now. You and Maximo are perfectly welcome. You're actually doing me a favor by staying there. We can talk later if this should blossom into a long-term arrangement but it will work itself out."

"How do things work themselves out in Hollywood?"

"They don't. Not usually. But, once in a long while, something special happens. That's what we show business people rely upon. We wait for something to happen. Then we develop and invest. With a little luck, everyone is happy."

"You think we're special?"

"Honey, I know you're special. And you tell me that your guy here is special."

"And you're willing to develop and invest in us?"

"Probably so. I'm pretty sure. But I don't know for sure until I know for sure."

"Oh, well, yeah…sure!"

Jimmy turned his attention to Maximo. He sipped his wine and looked Maximo over. He held up a finger to show he was thinking and about to say something. "Look, Maximo, I have faith in you already. You have this kind and thoughtful way about you. I see it already. But tell me, where do you see yourself in all of this?"

Maximo took a sip of his wine and also raised a finger. "I'm in a very interesting situation."

"Yeah, you're a duck out of water, right?"

"I don't know about that. I think we're all ducks in the same water."

"But you're going to need a brand. For example, there's the duck-out-of-water type. You could be this bumbling guy with a funny accent."

"No, that is the last thing I need to do! It would be so stupid and even dangerous to go around acting like a bumbling fool with a funny accent!"

Leslie leaned in close to Maximo, wishing she could whisper in his ear, she said in a low tone, "Come on, Maximo. Don't screw this up."

Jimmy gave them both a broad smile. "That's totally fine. I need to hear this. It gives me a taste of what's up ahead. It could work. A defiant comic, like a Jesuit priest!"

Maximo, encouraged, continued: "I have much to say. I will fill a niche."

"You will definitely fill a niche. Sometimes, it's a question of whether or not you're filling a niche anyone cares about. In your case, I know that people do care. Everyone is for the underdog."

"I'm more than an underdog." As if on cue, Rico popped his head up from Leslie's over-sized bag.

"Has he been here all along?" asked Jimmy.

"Of course, he has. We're not a magic act," blurted out Leslie and began to laugh.

"Back to my point," said Jimmy, "you can fill a niche, yes. You can inspire and you even educate. But don't forget the most important thing: You need to entertain!"

"We'll do that, Jimmy, don't you worry."

"Like I say, I'm not worried. I have nothing to worry about. And you have nothing to worry about. Just focus on the prize. Develop an act. Entertain. Do something!"

"We will, Jimmy!"

# 18

The new place on Venice Beach was cozy, very beachy with contemporary minimalist furniture and the obligatory framed poster print of Marilyn Monroe. Why Jimmy was holding off on turning it into an airbnb was beyond Leslie but she was happy to be grateful. The moment they got in the door, she planted a kiss on Maximo. "I think we're going to make history, Maximo!" To that, Maximo nodded and held Leslie tight. Then her phone chimed. She picked it up.

She motioned for Maximo to sit down, tried to cover the phone, and whispered, "It's John!" A few moments passed with Leslie pacing up and down and saying, "Yeah, uh huh," and "What the fuck!" Then a long silence and, finally, Leslie said, "He wants to talk to you."

Maximo did not want to talk to John but he took the phone. He could see John and it looked as if he was looking at a mirror. "I see you and it's so weird," said Maximo with genuine amazement.

"Yeah, dude. Same here, it's cool," sighed John. He even let out a little yawn.

"I think there's little doubt that we're related." Maximo tried to be as polite as he could be as he kept staring into the phone.

"I see that you've made yourself at home," said John and Maximo could clearly detect a smirk on John's face. He wasn't exactly trying to hide it.

"You have not had time to process any of this," said Maximo, with as much sympathy as he could muster.

"Look, Max, I don't hold anything against you."

"Really?"

"Yeah, I acted horribly. Leslie was right to do what she did. Who really knows what happens next. I'm open to whatever. I can only hope that she'll forgive me. All sorts of crazy shit happens and then things fall into place. You know, man, things happen."

This was an unexpected turn of events. What if Leslie was going to forgive John?

"Leslie," Maximo turned his attention to her. He was ready to beg for her answer. "You must still be feeling a bit overwhelmed." She nodded and held her eyes on him. She seemed to be gazing upon him. "Oh, Leslie."

"Max," John interrupted, "my man. You must be pretty overwhelmed yourself. You have gone from being a pampered Lothario to a man running towards redemption. That's quite a leap, some pretty heady stuff there. Talk about needing to process. It's like right out of a movie, dude!"

Dear God, what might have Leslie been saying to John?—and what does Leslie really think? Maximo was feeling none too easy. He knew he would have to answer for his sins, a combination of sloth and vanity. He understood he could have done so much more with his life by now. He had agonized over his lot in life as he grew older. After meeting Leslie, he let himself think that he might avoid confronting his past ever again and now this, being humiliated by John, his twin brother!

"Hey, man," John continued, "I'm willing to be up front about stuff. I've treated Leslie like crap. I'll be honest with you. I also don't think you're necessarily the solution—but I'm just throwing that out there. We're just two bros trying to keep it real, right? Just two bros having a little family reunion right here and right now, am I right?"

"John, you're my twin, right? That's weird but it's true."

"I know, dude. Isn't that wild?"

# 19

"We can't have him calling us all the time, Leslie. That's going to drive us crazy!" Maximo said this as calmly as possible. They had walked over to a nearby coffee shop as if walking out of the apartment would help them allude John.

"Hey, he can be texting me right now. Who knows, maybe he's already left me a new text," replied Leslie. It wasn't a taunt but just a statement of fact. "I know John. He's an asshole but he's not a psycho. I think, if we block him, that will piss him off and could escalate the situation. If we roll with it, he'll be satisfied that he can keep tabs on us, more or less. I'm going to remain neutral. I'm not going to encourage him."

"I'm so glad you're not going to encourage him!"

"Look, Maximo, we have a very hot and messy situation here. John's mind is still fuzzy on what he's going to do next. Our minds are still fuzzy too. If John gets pissed off, he could do a lot of damage.

I've still got all his ID and credit cards so he could report them stolen, although I seriously doubt it—I hope. He doesn't know what he wants or what I want. He could turn you in to ICE."

"He can turn me into ice?"

"No, ICE, the immigration Gestapo."

"Okay, I feel threatened---but not by you, Leslie. Are we on the run? I'm just feeling like this is turning into a Bonnie and Clyde thing with us."

"Are we running? Maybe we're walking very briskly. Anyway, that's one way to become famous."

"Bonnie and Clyde became infamous, big difference."

"Yeah, right. We're not going to hold up any banks either. We just need to stay calm."

Just then, Maximo picked up a pen and paper and did a quick little sketch. In fact, it was a little portrait of Leslie. She couldn't help but notice and began to study it. "Hey, I like that. You're good. Do you draw a lot? I guess the answer would be yes to that, huh? You're an artist."

"I do draw a lot. I have paintings back home. I regularly do sketches. I need to get a sketchbook. Some people need cigarettes. I need to do sketches."

"I hear ya. I quit smoking a while back. Sometimes I get an itch to smoke again and I do. I should take up drawing. That won't kill you."

"Drawing brings me to life. It is a part of me, part of my life."

"You know what, you can have a slide show of your art as part of your act. Just simple little drawings to help tell your story. You're one of these storyteller comedians. So, you can do well with some arty props."

"That's a great idea. When do you think we should do that?"

"I don't think we have any time to waste. Tonight?"

"You want to try to do something tonight?"

# 20

There wasn't enough time to set up a proper slide show so Leslie and Maximo got creative. They bought a big pad of paper, a marker and an easel so that Maximo could easily draw and display some drawings on stage. The low tech solution turned out to work really well.

"This is a drawing of my dog, Rico" Maximo stood next to it and the audience seemed to like it. He could hear some women in the back making sounds of approval. "He's a Chihuahua dog and he's very good company." There were a few snickers of laughter. "I'm Mexican so I sort of hesitated about sharing this. I don't want to come off as a stereotype. I do happen to be illegal." That triggered an uproar of laughs.

Maximo switched to the next page. It was a drawing of a hot air balloon. "Let me share with you some more. I crossed the border in a hot air balloon." Again, a big burst of laughs. "It's not the easiest way to cross the border. First, you need to get a hot air balloon. But it turned out to be a very smooth trip for most of the way." More laughs. It seemed Maximo just needed to maintain a steady pace and the audience was his.

"Let me tell you something. I have discovered that if I try to make friends, people can respond very positively." Maximo gestured for Leslie to join him on the stage. "This is a new friend of mine. Leslie, tell the audience how friendly I am."

Leslie, without missing a beat, answered, "Yeah, he doesn't deserve to be put in a cage. Nobody deserves to be put in a cage. It's kinky at best and disgusting and dangerous at worst. No one should be put in a cage unless they want to be put in a cage. That's just basic rules of consent. Our government is acting like an out-of-control racist sadist, if you ask me." More laughs.

"Things are very scary. All we can do is try to be friends. Leslie is my friend and I hope you'll be my friend too!" Time had run out and Maximo and Leslie left with a big round of applause. It was an impressive effort, especially since they were both still sleep-deprived and they had just managed to squeeze onto the open mic list.

As they walked off stage and headed toward the bar, they spotted Jimmy Gold. He was beaming a broad smile. "You guys did good, really good. If I didn't know any better, I'd say something lit a fire under you." Maximo and Leslie were excited to see Jimmy. It was a strange but wonderful coincidence but it was probably no surprise that Jimmy was always near and circulating. He nodded to them to follow him. They proceeded to walk down a hall that they hadn't noticed before. This led to an office tucked away in a dimly-lit corner. "Take a seat, guys." Maximo and Leslie were astonished to see a fully equipped meeting room done up with high end furnishings.

"I think we need to strike while the iron is hot. This is a combination of chemistry and luck. What Maximo lacks in experience he makes up for with solid instincts. What Leslie lacks in solid instincts she makes up for with her own set of skills. The two of you would do great breaking in an act, going on a little tour. It wouldn't be anything big at first. I would secure you get first priority on a bunch of open mics across the country and we'll see what happens. What do you think?"

If running to Hollywood had been the first answer to their problems, then actually running around the country like a Bonnie and Clyde comedy tour was the logical next step. "Of course we'll do it!" yelled Leslie. "Yes, I love it! Thank you, Jimmy," chimed in Maximo.

"Alright, it's settled. I'll set up a little spending allowance for you so you won't be beholden to that jerk, John, that Leslie has told me about. But you'll still need to be careful since Maximo is not exactly legal."

"I'm working on it!"

# 21

It was indeed going to be a bumpy ride: Maximo, Leslie, and John (via smartphone) all across the country. Jimmy had them covering a good cross-section. First stop was Houston; then a quick stop in New Orleans followed up by a lurching swing north to Rapid City, North Dakota; a visit to Chicago; then Columbus; then Philadelphia; then New York City; and Washington, D.C. to top it all off. It was sort of crazy and ambitious and exciting. Jimmy could give them even more tour stops but that seemed plenty to begin with. Jimmy didn't seem to be making any demands and he was paying for it, happy to experiment. And, unlike John, he wasn't monitoring their every move. Their mission was to survive the tour and, in the end, put together an act they could build on. Maximo felt as if he was being groomed yet again for something with a vague future.

"Let's get what we can out of this, Maximo," sighed Leslie, once they drove onto the freeway.

"I'm very grateful for your help in making me a star," said Maximo, unsure of what to say.

"Don't you worry about any of this, just like Jimmy said. I'm getting what I want out of it too. I make it look easy, as if I'm not even there. But I'm getting my stage time. I'm up there reciting lines when I need to be. And I'm behind the scenes too."

"It's so much work for you, Leslie."

"It is what it is. I'm not sure you realize how much work you're doing. This is all sort of new for you. A lot of what you're doing takes some guys years to build up the courage to do. Some never quite do it and instead keep planning on doing it. Most never get as far as you have already. It's not rocket science and yet, in a funny way, it is!" Just then there was a faint buzzing sound. "Oh shit, it's John."

It was not exactly a family reunion between John and Maximo the day before but, despite their differences, it could not be dismissed. John concluded that the two of them would need to start talking, no matter how awkward it might be. So, again, he asked Leslie if he could speak with Maximo.

"Hey, I'm all for giving something its due. It was pretty fucking awesome, in a very strange way, to meet you on the phone yesterday, even if you've been fucking my girl. Okay, that's not how I meant to start this. It's weird, you know?"

"Yes, under different circumstances, I think we'd be hugging each other. At least, I think we would be doing that. We're family. You know things. I know things. I imagine you are curious to know more about your past."

"Yeah, well, it's not really my past that I've been dying to discover. It's someone's past but I already know enough about my own life. Ancestry, all this shit about where you came from, it's all a bit over-rated, if you ask me."

"Come on, John," Maximo became irritated. "Don't be an asshole!"

John jumped at that. "Okay, chill out, dude!" He thought Maximo was going to remain all calm and quiet. "It sounds like you grew up with our mother. And I was meant to grow up with our father but then I got handed off to another guy."

"Isn't that right?" Maximo asked as respectfully as possible.

"Yeah. I don't like thinking about any of this. I grew up with a man who did his best to be a father to me. I've never really known him on a deep level and, similar to your case, he never spoke about either my birth mother or birth father."

"How strange. How very strange."

"Yeah, strange, isn't it? Or maybe it's more typical than you'd care to think. You're the romantic, Maximo. Look, things change. People move on. The man I grew up with knowing as my father, well, he remarried. I see him and his wife whenever I want. The cards have all been reshuffled. Everyone's in a whole different place."

"My mother never remarried. She remained this strange and distant figure frozen in time. It seemed as if little as possible changed. People moved as little as possible. Everything moved at a glacial pace, all in place, all in the same place and time. The building itself, that I grew up in, it went through renovations but nothing I ever took much notice of. Much simply remained the same, little activity."

"Such little activity can really hurt, Max." It irritated Maximo how casually John fell into calling him by a nickname. He wanted to say something but he didn't want to give John the satisfaction.

"I want to move about, John."

Just then, Leslie pointed at Maximo's new prized possession, that leather notebook from his father. "Maximo, talk to him about your book. It is supposed to be from your father." She kept pointing at it.

74

Maximo picked it up abruptly and it fell out of his hand and hit the floor of the car with a thud. An audible crack could be heard. "Did it split the spine?" It felt lose to the touch. Maximo suddenly noticed the endpaper had come undone. A business card fell out. "Hey, this was tucked inside."

Maximo lifted up the card. He read it aloud, so that John could hear:

*Williams & Williams*
*Attorneys at Law*
*575 Sycamore Circle*
*Charlottesville, Virginia*

"John," Maximo pleaded with him. "Does this mean anything to you?"

With more emotion than he had previously been willing to show, John answered, "Yeah, sure, that does mean something. That means a lot, Max. I think it could be the key to solving this whole crazy mess. How about that?"

## 22

John didn't have to reveal what he knew about Charlottesville. His reluctant yet genuine act of kindness, left Leslie feeling a bit empathetic towards him. The three of them seemed to have found themselves united in a common cause. "Guys," Leslie pleaded, "let's put our differences aside. Maybe we need to act more maturely. Maybe we need to go to Charlottesville."

"That's acting maturely? To run off to Charlottesville?" John's voice was so stern it almost sounded like he was actually there with them instead of just a voice on a phone.

"John, you said that address holds the key."

"I know. I know."

"What is the key, then?" asked Maximo, a little puzzled.

"I was always told that I was born in Virginia and that my first days or months were in Charlottesville," said John, "I was also led to believe that my true parents were unable to care for me. I was raised by a wealthy and powerful couple who had always wanted a son. The only thing was that they really weren't willing to put in the time to raise me themselves, directly. So, on paper, I was adopted by this wealthy couple and grew up in the D.C. area. It was a pleasant but restrained household. To be honest, I was mostly raised by the hired help. By the time I came of age, I was more than ready to move out. I never looked back. Unlike you, Max, I was the more adventurous type. I did return home to get a proper education but..."

"As I recall you telling me," Leslie interrupted, "you returned home quite a bit. And you stayed home quite a bit too. Not only that, your parents have a funny way of always being around, as if they hover around you, just waiting for you to retreat back to the nest."

"Alright, I won't dwell on those details. We're not doing a therapy session, are we? What I will say is that I think we could find out who this birth father is if we can go through the old archives at this law firm. I do recall Williams & Williams coming up from time to time in my stepfather's conversations when I was growing up. So, I give your little comedy tour my blessing. And make the last stop Charlottesville! Max, go out there and perform at comedy clubs and hone your act! At the end of the road, maybe there's a pot of gold or whatever."

"John, let me leave you with this idea: We do what we can."

"Do what we can, huh?"

"If I am misunderstood or ignored, whatever it might be, I can always say that I did what I could."

"Yeah, cool, Max. Maybe you're going against the odds. Maybe we've just uncovered a CIA plot and we don't even know it. Maybe you're JFK's love child. Whatever!"

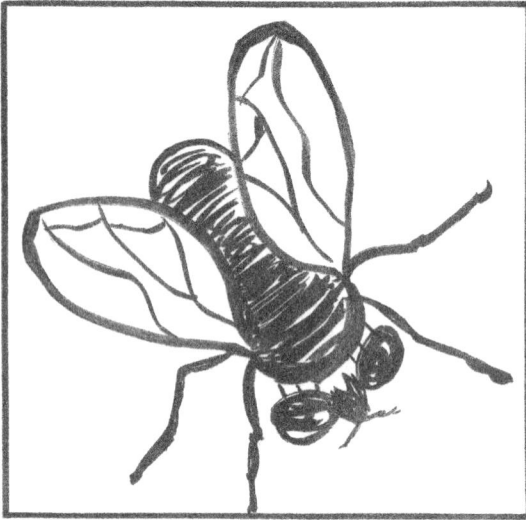

# 23

"Everybody knows somebody in Houston. But nobody knows Houston," said Leslie. She had gotten into a good zone on the road, driving with a sense of purpose as they eased their way to their first stop, Houston, Texas.

"You just thought of that?" asked Maximo.

"Yeah," said Leslie. She gave a little shrug. "Did you know that Houston is the original 'Emerald City'? They call Seattle that too. And that's because nobody cares or notices Houston! I mean no disrespect. That's just the luck of the draw, you could say. The Seattle people adopted the name, never bothered to check if it was already well established with another city. Houston is that other city! It's a big city, with its own history, but no drama. You don't have slogans or movies named after Houston."

"Well, there is that famous one, 'Houston, we have a problem,' from a NASA trip to the moon. One of the trips to the moon that wasn't making the headlines until they almost had a big accident, right? People should never have gotten jaded about going to the moon!"

"Sure. Anyway, Houston is one of these big cities without a face really. It has its sports. It has its museums. It has its night life. But you don't plan a dream vacation to Houston, do you? No, you don't. It's a big city, soaked in oil money, that is too big to fail and, despite its size, maintains a low profile. Don't mess with Texas."

"Yeah, is that phrase some sort of threat?"

"Sure, it could be. Actually, it comes from an anti-litter campaign. So, that's your profile on Houston. Big. Anonymous in a lot of ways. Wants to be left alone. Sort of just a smaller version of the whole country."

"But is it part of the Land of Trump? Are we entering Trump Country?"

"I don't know. I really don't know. Houston is so big that it can accommodate red, blue, and purple. On the face of things, it definitely leans conservative. But, just like the rest of the country, the Land of Trump is such a mixed brew that spills into places like toxic waste so whatever is considered 'Trump country,' is a very murky thing.

Houston, like so much of the country, is made up of suburbs. Folks hold their cards close to their vest in the burbs. It can get quite mysterious. But, with the way that Trump has been behaving, well, looks to me like quiet low-key places like Houston may have had just about enough and are ready for a big change."

"Okay, well, that definitely puts things into perspective!"

"Got any new jokes you're working on?"

"I was just thinking about that. I read that twelve people can fit in the torch carried by the Statue of Liberty. That's pretty impressive. I don't think you can walk all the way up into the torch but, if you did, there's room for twelve. Like, say, the Supreme Court could fit up in there. That would be pretty cool if they all got up in the torch and declared that, from now on, all their decisions would be genuinely fair and, without a doubt, follow the rule of law."

"You think that observation is good for a laugh?"

"It could be."

That night, Maximo made some quirky remarks regarding the Statue of Liberty and it got some good laughs. It was worth it but it probably still needed some work.

Leslie and Maximo found a hotel, a good one but not so posh that it might seem to be taking advantage of the Jimmy Gold expense account. They needed to choose carefully and pace themselves. That said, they still managed to get a nice view of Buffalo Bayou, which snaked through the city and could put rivers to shame during a flash flood. The two of them just stared out from the balcony. Maximo searched around but could not spot even one cowboy hat. If he didn't know any better, he was staring out at some city anywhere on the planet.

"These are good people out here. Honest. Hard-working. Good people. They just want to be left alone. For the most part, they're not bothering anyone and they don't want to be bothered. I know. I have family out here and they don't want to know about me."

"You should have said something, Leslie. Don't you want to see them?"

"I have a sister out here but, believe me, she doesn't want to talk. I don't want to get into it. It's better this way. It helps me understand a big city like Houston. I can tell you that much."

# 24

That very next morning, they made it to New Orleans. The big city vibe of Houston gave way to a more mellow as well as more flavorful scene. This was New Orleans, a city of mystery and charm. Maximo knew this place was like no other. It had to do with a special character that had emerged from the horror of slavery; the struggle for freedom; and the defiance needed to remain free. Here was a big spirit that was simply not going to be suppressed. A big beautiful spirit that brought Creoles and Cajuns together. Maximo had read about New Orleans and taken it all to heart, including one particular connection that often crossed his mind. New Orleans was the birth place of one of the most celebrated cartoonists of all time, George Herriman, the creator of the *Krazy Kat* comic strip. Only after his death did it become known that Herriman was of mixed race, part Anglo and part African American. It explained a lot about the complexity found in one of America's earliest, and most significant, comic strips.

Maximo and Leslie had gotten a table at Café Du Monde and settled down for a traditional midday snack of coffee and beignets, those puffy fried fritters blanketed in powdered sugar. Maximo made a point of stopping by the hotel newsstand and picked up the latest issue of *The New Yorker*. He showed it to Leslie. "You can't imagine how difficult it is to get a cartoon accepted by this magazine."

"Oh, I know, Maximo. Are you trying to tell me that you're in this issue?"

"They accepted a cartoon of mine and it's supposed to be in this issue. What with everything that's been happening lately, I lost track. But this is it! Let me see now, it could be anywhere." He fumbled through the pages, furiously leafing back and forth, plucking out subscription cards as he went along. "Wait. Uh, yes, here it is!" Giving it one more look of admiration, he turned the page around so that Leslie could see too.

The cartoon was an oversized dog seated in a plush club chair as he read a newspaper, complete with reading glasses. Two people stood nearby. One person said to the other: "I can't believe he still enjoys reading the newspaper!"

Leslie was impressed, even overjoyed. "This is insane! I've never known an actual *New Yorker* cartoonist! It looks so good, Maximo!"

Maximo rubbed his forehead, as if in deep thought. "It's a rare gift to have what it takes to grace the pages of *The New Yorker*! I didn't know if I really had it in me." He realized how pretentious that sounded but he didn't care.

"Well, you don't need to be validated. But, at the same time, it is really trippy!"

And then, of course, Leslie's phone went off. It was John. Just another quick call. Sure, nothing to worry about. "Maximo was just showing me a cartoon of his that is in this week's *New Yorker*!"

Maximo shook his head, pleading with Leslie not to say anything more. But the big news had already been let out. Leslie looked at Maximo with a quizzical look. "John is wondering if you won the caption contest too. That's the one he cares about. Sorry, that's John for you!"

Maximo wondered what sort of humor John really liked and if he was even capable of truly being funny. How did someone like Leslie ever get involved with him? What the hell was his appeal other than his shallow and pathetic need to dominate? There was something annoyingly artificial, downright robotic, about John's sense, or lack of sense of humor. It was more of a competitive game for him than an attempt at levity or wit. Maximo wondered if most Americans shared this same inane trait and then suddenly concluded that John probably wasn't alone at all. Westerners, and especially Americans, had a fetish for shallow bite-sized bits of snark. Didn't he already have mountains of proof of that from the internet, social media and cable news? Everyone fancied themselves a comedian, a pundit, a superstar. Civility had gone out the window years ago. Patience had gone out the window years ago. And common sense had gone out the window years ago. John was an asshole but he was far from alone. People embraced that mindset. People were more likely to check out and vegetate than put in the effort to attempt to do anything remotely remarkable. That's what Maximo wanted to say to as big an audience as possible of these like-minded people. But, no, he wasn't going to do that. He didn't even dare say this to Leslie! And even what he did dare to say was potentially more than enough to get his teeth knocked out. It didn't take much. So, he stewed as Leslie finished her call and settled back down. "He says he's very proud of you."

"Proud of me? Who does he think he is? My dad?" He stopped himself. He took in a deep breath and cleared his mind. When he let out a deep sigh, it came to him. "You know, I need to appeal to people's better nature--even if it sometimes doesn't appear to exist at all."

"How will you do that?"

"I'm going to try to be a little more gentle, even whimsical. But not silly and stupid. I'm going to try an experiment. George Herriman is a favorite son of New Orleans. I should do something in his honor."

"Who is George Herriman?" asked Leslie, a bit baffled.

"He's the creator of the *Krazy Kat* comic strip."

"Krazy what?"

"It's a shame but most people don't know—or at least not right away. Don't you remember ever seeing an old-timey comic strip with a mouse hurling a brick at a cat?"

"I can't say that I have."

"It wasn't known during his lifetime but George Herriman was biracial, half white and half black. He started out his career at the turn of the last century, when it wasn't safe going around telling folks you were of mixed race. Maybe he never would have left New Orleans to seek his fortune if he'd been upfront about his racial makeup. If he and his family had been candid, maybe they would never have survived living in New Orleans way back then. Anyway, after a number of false starts, Herriman hit upon a comic strip that revolved around a cat and a mouse, as well as a dog. It was surreal, sophisticated, and appealed to everyone. And, along with all the slapstick comedy, Herriman got to make a number of comments on race, as if speaking out in a special code. Krazy Kat, for instance, was always concerned about being black and made various attempts to turn white!"

"The cartoon cat wanted to be as while as his creator! Oh, how cute? Sounds pretty sad to me," sighed Leslie.

"It was a very different time, more twisted than our own!"

"We're living in some pretty twisted times right now. Maybe a cat and a mouse speaking in code would fit right in. They could be

84

pretending to help build a wall while, the whole time, they keep hiding the bricks. Yeah, that would be funny!"

"Yeah, something as simple as that could be very funny."

And so they tried that very same joke that night and people laughed. They seemed to laugh more at that than the Statue of Liberty joke. In the end, they decided to keep both jokes in the act and move forward.

The trip down to New Orleans had taught Leslie and Maximo both that some places are just more open and honest than other places. New Orleans wasn't Seattle, that was for sure! It wasn't built to be frosty polite. It was too hot and humid for that to begin with. And it had experienced too much in the way of blood, sweat and tears to ever live in a bubble. When Leslie and Maximo mentioned Seattle, no one looked down on them either. It seemed that most folks enjoyed providing that famous Southern hospitality. And when Maximo found himself using that cautious and respectful-sounding term, "African American," he was kindly corrected by a young couple at a bar. They promptly said, "Nah man, just say black. It's okay. Just say black."

There was no need to tiptoe over anything. Anyone who was decent and forthright would tell you that. There was no other way but to keep it real.

# 25

That very night, Maximo had a lucid dream that carried him back to Mexico City. If he was a stranger in a strange land in the United States, he could recall a time and place where he was completely in his element. It didn't take all that much to make him feel at ease. It could be something simple to nourish his soul and soothe his ego on a nice summer day. He was completely content to haunt one of his favorite Norte Roma cafes and spend much of the day writing down observations, reading a novel, and sketching. It was on just one of those sort of days that he'd come up with the cartoon of the dog reading a newspaper, the very same cartoon that made it into the pages of *The New Yorker*.

He could see it now. No sooner had he finished drawing the dog reading a newspaper  and set it down than a pretty young woman admired it. She had given Maximo the sweetest smile. He looked over to her, seated so close to him, and he couldn't help but admire her smooth legs and pretty feet. He returned to her face: her soft brown skin, her dark brown eyes, her full lips. Her name was Amelia and she was also an artist.

She was sitting at her favorite spot for coffee, Boicot Cafe. It was the same old crowd. It was a steamy summer day. She had the whole world before her. Then she meets Maximo. She had her legs crossed with one foot pointed directly at him. She noticed him looking at her foot and wiggled her toes. Maximo, not missing a beat, said, "An ionized environment really helps, you know."

Well, she'd heard just about everything there was to hear during her cafe stays. She liked the sound of Maximo's voice. It wasn't a whiny hipster sound. It wasn't arrogant. It wasn't stale. What it was was pleasant. She wondered what he'd say next, just for fun.

She flexed her toes in anticipation, then scrunched them up, and finally relaxed her toes.

"It's the healthy negative ions that feed our cells," Maximo continued. And, yes, sure enough, he was confident. But what was he talking about anyway?

"There is no way to avoid the toxic electromagnetic fields. EMFs are emitted from all our gadgets. Wi-Fi, computers and cell phones aren't going away. And what do you get for your loyalty to technology, to the status quo? Stress. Memory loss. Tumors. Brain damage. Why are we even having this conversation, right?" Maximo was on a roll. "You won't get cancer anytime soon. It will gradually creep up on you," he went on with a heavy sigh.

She looked at him and he caught her gaze. They examined each other as if they were the last two humans left on Earth and, by the way he was talking, she could easily feel that way.

"What are you doing for the Apocalypse?" she asked.

"I do have a solution," he said.

"But you said we can't avoid all that harmful radiation."

"It's all around us, that's true."

He walked up to her. He stood over her. She leaned in, waiting for a response. She was in a relaxed pose, legs still crossed, her foot dangling in front of him. He gently bowed and held her exposed bare foot. She did not resist. It felt so natural.

"The solution is right under our feet. Your feet need to be grounded to the Earth. In that way, you are receiving the natural and healthy negative ions emitted from the Earth."

"I'm barefoot most of the time. I mostly wear flip flops."

"Then you are on the right path. But it has to be direct contact with the Earth to get the full benefits."

"I agree. Boy, you're quite passionate about this but I don't blame you. I think we're all headed for disaster but we'd rather pretend nothing's wrong."

"Everything's wrong. It's hard to resist, the reality we've created for ourselves."
He looked away for a moment, as if to catch his breath and collect his thoughts.

"And every step we take back to nature, is a step back to basics, back to our true selves, healthy and sound." She was on a roll. She was proud of herself, and she meant every word.

"I like the sound of your voice." He surprised himself. He suddenly felt vulnerable.

"I like the sound of yours!"

He nodded with approval and recognition as he pulled up a chair to sit right at her table.

"You know, they say with enough salt lamps you can effectively counter the effect of EMFs in your home."

"Yeah, there's that. There's all sorts of products, now that I think of it. I see some of them in that New Age shop around the corner."

"Well, it would take a lot of steps away from the status quo to break free and be more in tune with yourself. It wouldn't be easy, at first, to dismantle this trap."

"You know, this place has really excellent Wi-Fi."

"I know. Isn't that terrible?"

"Depending on how you look at it, yes, it's pretty atrocious."

By now, Maximo was feeling quite soothed and nourished by the turn of events. Amelia seemed so natural and generous of spirit. When she suggested he go home with her, he was pleasantly surprised. Wasn't he too old to be embarking upon one-nighters? Well, who was to say what would happen? Maybe she considered herself too old to still be playing the ingénue. So, he agreed to do as she asked and followed her home, which turned out to be a nice short walk from the café.

She actually took him home to show him her etchings, as they say in romance novels. Well, it was a book of sketches, and actually quite nice: ambitious work by a raw talent. There was something about her love for pottery. She had a genuine interest in still life themes.

They didn't roll into bed right away either. Maximo insisted that they watch a Marx Brothers movie. Amelia actually liked it. Maximo couldn't resist sharing *Duck Soup* with her. It was so subversive and silly and maybe gave her another look into his sensibility. She chuckled over Chico's line: "Who are you going to believe, me or your own eyes?" And then she got on top of him and started kissing him. Maximo marveled over those soft kisses. He came back with kisses that were a little harder and longer. She liked that. Before Groucho could come back and steal the screen with another punch line, they had departed to the back bedroom.

Maximo was quite charmed by Amelia. She was just south of thirty but still quite girlish and innocent. It took them a while longer than expected before they got out of their clothes. It had been her idea, after all? He let it all play out gradually. She pressed him towards her and gave herself over to him fully, without any further hesitation. Maximo had a grateful smile on his face. He kissed her again harder and longer. "Place your weight on me," she said. He complied. "Don't forget a condom," she said. Then she turned to her nightstand and fumbled through a drawer. As she stretched over to get the condom, she raised a leg and strategically placed a foot on his chest. "Hold that thought," she said and let out a little gasp of delight.

Everything began to suddenly blur. His dream was fading away. Where did Amelia go? She had been right there with him, holding him, kissing him, caressing him. She'd invited him to spend the night. That had already been arranged, right? But now, all of a sudden, a fog had descended upon this happy, most fortunate, coupling. It was over all too soon. He was waking up to a new day. He was no longer in Mexico City, sipping a latte or bedding a beauty. He was no longer in his element. He was back in the United States. A new day had begun.

# 26

Now came the hard part: heading north all the way to Mount Rushmore. Apparently, this gig was connected to one of Jimmy Gold's most beloved old cronies. Maximo and Leslie were tempted to call it off but there was something alluring about that crusty ole national monument and being away from it all. Then it occurred to Maximo that, since they were already sort of heading in that direction, they might as well pass through Monument Valley, the setting for all the *Krazy Kat* comic strips! Leslie didn't quite agree but she warmed up to it. She was more of a city girl but, in the end, it was one of those bucket list moments too good to pass up. And Maximo had really become very anxious about it. He was very pumped up about going to Monument Valley.

"This isn't exactly the best time and place to tell you about another artist who means a lot to me but, at the same time, it is." Maximo obviously wanted to confide something to Leslie.

"Another artist that you admire? Okay, I'm all set," said Leslie in the most inviting tone she could muster. She'd already taken care of all the details in repacking. Rico was in the back seat with a fresh chew toy. It was time to listen to the tortured soul that was Maximo.

"I was force fed a bowl of Basquiat each day by my mother before I even had a chance to decide for myself whether or not I liked his work. My memory is foggy, or I try not to think about it. But, what happened was that my mother became quite obsessed with Jean-Michel Basquiat. She followed contemporary art and she convinced herself that I was every bit as talented. Basquiat and I were actually around the same age. It's funny to think about. I'm around the age he would be now if he were still alive today. Back when we were both young men, my mother badgered me about Basquiat all the time! She demanded that I do my own version of his Art Brut paintings. I made some half-hearted attempts under duress. In fact, his style is very accessible as far as I'm concerned. I had no problem emulating him but I wasn't going to follow anyone's strict orders for very long, especially not my wacko mother's orders!"

"I'm so sorry to hear this. It sounds like an artist's nightmare!" Leslie was genuinely horrified. Poor Maximo had spent too long stewing in a hot pot of art gumbo! If she could help him finally make his mark, she was determined to do her best.

"Exactly! You can't order someone to start dancing as fast as they can just because you want them to! It doesn't work that way. You can come close to killing that person's love for this or that artist. You can come close to killing that person, period!"

"Your mother was a piece of work."

"Of all people, why did she have to obsess over Basquiat! I did not need her to push me to like his work. I had no problem with him until my mother almost soured me on him."

"So, you bring all this up now because…"

"Yes, I bring all this up because I do still want to channel Basquiat, at least on my own terms. I've been thinking quite a lot about him recently, in connection with Herriman. Think of it. These were two great American misfits: African American artists fighting for their place at the table. Both of them working at times of great racial conflict. Neither man was welcome on the grounds of race. One man hid his race. The other was defiant. Both men created art full of coded messages about race. They raged through codes messages!"

"Alright, I see where you going with this. So, you'd like to speak to that in your own art."

"Of course I do! I'm already doing it. I'm doing it as we speak. I need to keep drawing all the way to Monument Valley! Don't stop. Keep driving. And I'll keep drawing!"

Maximo was so insistent and that sort of excited Leslie. She'd do it. She'd keep driving. Helping an impassioned artist really turned her on. Who knew, she might be able to completely break it off from John and never look back. But she wasn't completely there yet. For now, she could lose herself in Maximo's mad quest.

"This is my own obsession, mama! Nobody else's!" Maximo let out a shrill little laugh. And so it went. He drew like crazy: pictograms, mice, cats, dogs, notes, symbols, various observations and calculations. And she drove, a little crazy, but not too much.

Every time that Leslie was brave enough to sneak a look, she'd see Ignatz or Krazy Kat or Officer Pup moving along at full tilt upon the page. Bricks were flying this way and that way. Crosshatching would overcome one page followed by delicate ethereal drawings on a spare background on another page. Each and every time they'd stop at a rest stop, Maximo would bring his sketchbook close to his chest and stare out. Leslie would yank his arm and he'd relent and let her take a quick look at a page or two. Finally, at one rest stop not too far from their final destination, Maximo let go and handed the sketchbook over to Leslie.

"You know, it's fascinating how George Herriman managed to navigate through the culture of the time back at the start of the last century. It was an oppressive time when white men were in charge and, bit by bit, things have improved over the last hundred years or so. But those bits aren't quite finished changing, are they?"

"Keep dancing, Maximo. Keep dancing to your own tune."

# 27

That next morning was exceptionally cozy as they'd found a wonderful spot of solitude right in the thick of it all. They could clearly see the famous Monument Valley Mitten rock formations, what looked like two mammoth god-like hands, shooting out from the ground and raised toward the heavens. Maximo sensed this could be the last relaxed and mellow morning for the two of them in a long time.

The collection of drawings that Maximo had created told the story of Ignatz and Kray Kat, if they lived in the present era, in the age of Trump. Apparently, these two had seen worse and gone through worse. They begin by making one little sly comment after another. Then they observe Officer Pup busily rounding up all sorts of other critters that are deemed undesirable. Oh, they're just a bunch of Others that need to be hauled away! But why can't they stay even if when they have legitimate reasons and have followed all the rules? Well, the Big Bad Boy in the Big Bad White House doesn't care for their kind. Oh, I see. And so it went. In the end, Ignatz and Krazy promised to help build a wall to keep out all the Others but they decided to hide all the bricks instead. In due time, and time has a way of coming due, the Big Bad Boy was never heard from again!

Would George Herriman have created something like what Maximo had just done? Perhaps so. Maximo had been faithful to the absurdity and surrealism in *Krazy Kat*.

"I think George Herriman did everything he could as an artist living in a world where up was down and down was up. He was a man hiding the fact he was half black in a country that just wasn't ready to accept him and, in some parts of the country, might be open to killing him. How do you survive, let alone create art, in that kind of environment?" asked Maximo. And then he looked around at where he was. "What you do is find a way to transcend the horror and limitations. You find a place just like this. You go to Monument Valley!"

Maximo and Leslie stood there enjoying the wide open space. They may as well have been on Mars. It was such an otherworldly terrain. No room for anything but natural splendor. No room for glib and hurtful remarks. No room for racism. No room for anything but magnificent peace and quiet.

Maximo gathered up and neatly stacked the pages he'd been working on. He especially liked the one where he put a Basquiat crown on the head of Ignatz. It all made sense and he knew he would now have Basquiat's urgent notes and Ignatz and Krazy Kat all dancing in his head for the rest of this road trip.

Having accomplished what he set out to do, a drawing marathon culminating at Monument Valley, Maximo wanted to indulge in another long hard look at his father's journal. He dug it out of his backpack. In his haste, and with the crazy turn of events, he still had much to look over. There was this wild drawing of an Aztec god that left him wondering. Could it be that his father, whoever he was, also had a need to create a secret language of his own?

So, with Monument Valley surrounding him, Maximo took a moment to savor his father's carefully rendered drawing of the Aztec rain god, Tlolac. Such a fine piece of work! His father had captured the ferocity of that fanged monster while including some delicate touches to suggest whimsy. This was definitely not something done as an afterthought. There was some kind of story behind it, but what? It even looked like it was a study drawn from the actual headstone what with the bits of shadow under the nose and around the base. Was it from a museum or out in the field somewhere? What exactly was his father doing in Mexico anyway?

"Oh, that's pretty, or should I say, pretty intense?" asked Leslie as she studied the drawing of Tlolac and placed a furtive arm around her newly decisive Hamlet.

"Pretty intense, that's for sure."

"I'm really happy right now." Leslie tightened her hold on him.

"It's all pretty crazy. This whirlwind tour that we're on and, at any moment, you-know-who might give you a call." Maximo suddenly regretted his curt comments but held his ground.

"Oh, who would that be?" Leslie backed away a step.

"Who do you think, Winston Churchill? Yeah, that's who would be calling you."

"How do I rate a call from Winston Churchill?"

So, she wanted to remain in denial about John. Maximo could only shrug. Then he kneeled down and picked up Rico, who was always handy. Maximo cradled Rico for a while and then rubbed his belly to which Rico let himself go as if awaiting nirvana.

# 28

Maximo and Leslie had forged onward and finally to Mount Rushmore. It had been an orgy of natural splendor leading up to America's most recognizable and most admired work of art. In other words, it was a colossal letdown after all they'd seen and experienced a few hours ago but, like a train wreck, they couldn't take their eyes off it. "They all look so clean and pristine," observed Leslie as she leaned into Maximo. She remained affectionate and Maximo had relented on being distant and difficult. That sort of drama was hardly going to get him anywhere anyway.

"These are the top four presidents in my book. All four are the gold standard," quipped Maximo. "They all make up the American ideal. I never thought much about this monument but it serves its purpose very well: it encourages you to go out and do something, even if that something is to make fun of it. At least all four of these guys were sane, well-read, and fairly reasonable. Not too much to ask from the leader of the free world."

That night, Maximo would be performing in a solidly red state. "I wonder what a Rapid City audience will be like," said Maximo.

Leslie edged up close. "I wouldn't go too fast and loose with the anti-Trump rhetoric in this neck of the woods, I'm just saying."

"Thanks for the advice, Leslie."

Maximo was feeling a bit reckless and decided to not heed Leslie's warning. After strolling through for a bit, Rapid City seemed pretty friendly. Perhaps it was a healthy mix of political opinion. So, it wasn't long before Maximo turned up the heat and some in the crowd started turning on him.

"As I see it, letting Trump be Trump is not helping anyone but Trump."

The hostility in the air was palpable and, if Maximo was tuning into his audience, he should have felt it.

"Really, I believe in every one of you. I just wonder what any of you see in someone full of empty promises and who is most concerned about himself. If you were on a date with Donald Trump, you would be running away by now. To better appreciate what it means for Trump to run this country, just think of your most dysfunctional relative suddenly in charge of your whole family."

There was the loud screech of chairs pulling back as people started to leave. People were leaving and not afraid to be less than quiet about it. "I love you guys. This is a confusing time with all these alternative facts floating around. Alternative facts are as bad as fake news. It all makes you want to throw up."

Some in the crowd began to boo him off the stage and Maximo made one last pointed remark. "Did you ever wonder if any elected official ever questioned the legitimacy of the press as much as Trump? You would need to go back to Stalin and Hitler. They both loved to call the press, 'The enemy of the people.' Trump says that all the time. Well, you can see for yourself, right?"

"You better go now, ya here?" yelled a man with a profound beer belly.

"Go where?" taunted Maximo. In response, this man, who would never have thought to do a sit-up was suddenly climbing on stage to get at Maximo. It was time to run and that's what Maximo did. He kept on running. Leslie and Maximo jumped into the trusty Subaru and drove off. Thankfully, the two of them survived without a scratch and it looked like no one was too eager to pursue them.

"Maximo, let's chill out, for real. Getting rough on Trump is going to get us killed!"

Maximo nodded. "I've had my fill. I think I've crossed the line as far as I can go."

They drove in silence for a while. It was pitch black, or so it seemed, until they bothered to just look up at the stars. A peaceful moment quickly passed at the sight of a billboard, bright red backdrop with white letters: "Make America Great Again!" Then the sign did a crazy thing. It suddenly became peppered with little black splotches, one after the other. The darkness overwhelmed the bright red and white empty slogan. The sign was instantly covered black. Leslie stared closely and then gasped. "It's covered in locusts!"

They drove in silence for another long stretch.

"Where does this disconnect come from?"

"America has always had problems and always will. What keeps things moving forward is competent leadership. Do we have that right now? Well, do we? I don't think so."

"You know the kind of leadership I'd like to see?" Maximo perked up. "Remember the movie, 'Giant'? That scene towards the end with Rock Hudson in the diner, you know what I'm referring to?"

Leslie shook her head at Maximo in an almost dismissive way but Maximo carried on. "Well, if you haven't seen it, the whole movie is building up to this one crucial moment. Rock Hudson is the patriarch of this big Texas family empire. All his life, he's been intolerant or dismissive of Mexicans. Never had a place for them in his heart. It's now the 1950s and his son has married a Mexican woman and they have a son. Well, Rock is there in this diner with his whole immediate family and an altercation breaks out which compels him to get involved. Basically, Rock has to stand up to the diner's owner who, just having harassed a Mexican family, has set his sights on Rock and his own mixed race family. A hard-knuckle fight ensues. Both the racist and Rock are bloody. Everything has exploded to the surface."

Leslie gave a quick nod.

"You know what I'm talking about, don't you, Leslie?"

Leslie seemed to straighten up in her seat. "I do. That scene gets me every time."

"Really, Leslie, you're moved by this scene?"

"Oh, yeah, I'm human. It's enough to get me crying."

"I'm glad to know this."

"Well, Maximo, I think that diner scene has worked its Hollywood magic on me. It rings more true now than in a long time."

"Just because of some political hacks who decided to stir up a heavy dose of hate."

# 29

The next day, they were in Illinois. In a lot of respects, Chicago was like Seattle, very blue and sure of itself.

They settled into a diner near the University of Chicago. Medici on 57th served a nice selection of comfort food and had a laid back atmosphere. A couple of gargoyles munching on hamburgers greeted customers from atop an arched entrance. And everywhere you looked, there were photographs and memorabilia honoring former President Barack Obama. Maximo couldn't help himself and began writing in his notebook as the waitress served coffee.

"The grub here is the best. I studied here with Second City and we'd come here for the grilled ham and cheese sandwiches," said Leslie with a sigh.

"You studied at Second City? Wow, that's impressive. Do you think I'm worthy of doing even a brief set on a Second City stage tonight?" asked Maximo, feeling a bit self-conscious for asking.

"Well, the students are very young. That's not to say it's ever too late to start doing comedy." Thanks both to Jimmy Gold and to Leslie, Maximo had secured a slot for that night. "In your case, you have no time to worry about what could have been. We have to work with who you are now and what you've already learned. You did workshops in Mexico, right?"

"Yes, I did. But I know about Second City. That's the gold standard for comedy. Bill Murray. Tina Fey. All the greats went through Second City. It's a Saturday Night Live hall of fame."

"I went there and took comedy classes right out of college. But, you know, it's really true what they say: No one can teach you to be funny. A lot of it is hype and people crawling over each other to get what they want. In the end, either you're funny or you're not. You can be somewhat successful but still not be all that funny or talented."

"I didn't mean to upset you."

"I'm not upset. I'm just looking forward to a ham and cheese. So, what are you working on?"

"I want to talk a little about history. I'm still working on it. History is very messy."

"Are you, nuts? That's what you're going to do tonight? History does not exactly guarantee belly laughs."

"I don't always have to be so funny."

"I noticed that."

"This is an opportunity to educate too. Despite popular belief, Christopher Columbus was far from a hero. He slaughtered many natives. Cortez killed many people too. He wiped out all the Aztec people. All kinds of explorers and settlers have killed natives."

"Okay, this is some pretty heavy shit to unload."

"Ninety percent of indigenous people were killed in the Americas from 500 years of European colonization. Maybe some got sick from new European diseases. Most got murdered."

"I hate to burst your bubble but talk of genocide usually doesn't go over so well with a comedy club's two-drink minimum."

"They don't teach this in high schools."

"Maybe not in high schools. But in prep schools they touch on it."

"Oh, really? So, if you come from a prosperous family with a guarantee of college in your future, then it's alright to know some real history. Maybe it comes in handy in the essay portion of an entrance exam. Knowledge is divided up between the rich and the poor."

"I didn't say that. Although that's basically...what I said."

"Aha, for some students, it is believed they cannot afford to know how the world really works!"

"Oh, I see that fire in your eyes. Tell me you're not going to go full throttle controversial on your audience tonight, Maximo! Remember, this is Second City, the Saturday Night Live hall of fame."

"Well, I'm not planning to. I can only promise it will be interesting!"

"Hard to say how a full-on Maximo, all fiery and idealistic, will play in Chicago. You're on your own."

Maximo bravely took the stage that night and stumbled his way into something interesting.

Maximo decided to bring up the ousting of Sen. Al Franken for allegations of sexual harassment. "I can see why Democrats would gang up on one of their own, Senator Franken. He was stupid. He crossed the line. But don't stop there. Take that same energy and push harder on Trump!"

Someone stood up and yelled, "What the hell do you think we're doing?"

Maximo shrugged, "I think you need non-stop protest in the streets."

The heckler pounced on that remark: "What is your problem?!"

"Everyone here is very high minded but just a bit too polite to ever get anything done. You did manage to kick Al Franken out of the Senate, which was cool but not enough."

"You're a fascist!" yelled out an otherwise passive-looking man. He looked like he'd just been awoken from a long nap but now he was relying on whatever stored up energy he had in him and was running towards the stage. A few other docile-turned-aggressive combatants joined in.

Maximo retreated, signaled Leslie, and they made a hasty exit. Before anyone could ever reach them, they'd already made it out the back exit.

"Maximo, how dare you speak ill of Al Franken right in the Saturday Night Live holy temple! He's one of their most beloved saints."

"But he's no saint."

"I know, but it doesn't matter."

Just then, Leslie turned around and nearly screamed. There, before them, was the one man they never expected to see. John gave them both a broad smile. "Hey there, guys. I know it's a shock but just roll with it, please. Welcome me into the fold."

To Maximo's shock and dismay, Leslie followed John's command and gave him a big hug. Where did that come from? Had they been texting all this time behind his back?

Leslie, with a sheepish grin, went back to Maximo to pull him into the new happy trio. She whispered into his ear, "Roll with it, baby. I called him and I think it's time we all worked together."

Maximo was upset but pulled himself together. He reached over and patted John's back in an attempt to replace the obligatory hug. John, without missing a beat, said, "Hey, it's okay, bro. The cavalry has arrived. I'm here to help, not hurt. Unless, of course, there's any reason to hurt."

# 30

The addition of John had a very strange effect on everyone, including John. When John found an opening during his texting with Leslie, he grabbed it. She had suggested that he join them and so he got on the first flight to Chicago. He had moved so fast, nearly teleporting himself, that his head was still spinning. For Maximo, it was difficult to get too angry when in the presence of John since it was like looking in a mirror. Leslie was more conflicted than ever with two nearly identical lovers in such close proximity. John was where he liked to be, in the driver's seat, and quite literally. Leslie was exhausted and had gratefully handed over the keys and perhaps too much responsibility over to him. The three of them, so suddenly, seemed to be making it work.

"Are we deep into the land of Trump?" asked Maximo, as they crossed into Ohio. He had gotten into the habit of asking that question in a playful manner with Leslie and now couldn't break the habit like an annoying tic.

As if on cue, The Pretenders played on the radio what had become known as *The Ohio Song*, aka, *My City Was Gone*. It was peppered with just the right amount of irresistible irony from lead singer Chrissie Hynde: "*I went back to Ohio. But my city was gone. There was no train station. There was no downtown.*" Everyone took a pause to let the quirky and defiant lyrics sink in. Just then, a tall and lanky figure could be seen up ahead. He stuck his thumb out to hitch a ride and looked every inch like the loopy hitchhiker in *Fear and Loathing in Las Vegas*. John set his eyes hard on him for a beat. "Hey, you think we should give this guy a lift?"

Maximo and Leslie both just stared at the mysterious stranger up ahead. The closer they got, the more bookish and unthreatening he appeared. "Okay, we can give it a try," said Leslie. "But it's on you, John. If he starts to act weird, he's your responsibility!" John shrugged.

The car came to a stop just a few feet ahead of the hitchhiker. John signaled for him to hop in and the young and scruffy man came into full view. He looked intelligent and even a bit delicate, as if he wasn't meant to be outdoors for very long. He ran up to the car sort of funny too, very animated and uncoordinated. "Oh, thank you so much! I can't believe my luck! Hello, I'm Brad! So glad to meet you!" Instantly, they now had a new visitor on the road with them. And, all the while, Chrissie Hynde sang about the woeful state of an overdeveloped Ohio. "Oh, I love that song! What timing too. That is the perfect song for you guys, travelling through these parts. Are you visiting Ohio, I'm guessing?"

John volunteered a few quick facts: "We're passing through. We don't know much about Ohio, except for what we know from this Pretenders song! I'm John. This is Maximo. This is Leslie." Everyone nodded and smiled.

"So, are you passing through as well?" asked Maximo.

To this, Brad jumped in with an eager reply: "You can say that I'm passing through this whole country! I'm on a fact-finding journey of sorts. It all began with my blog. I fancy myself a good judge of character, a good observer and commentator. One thing led to another and I found myself writing about seeking out what is going on in this country."

"And what is going on in this country, Brad?" asked Leslie with genuine concern.

Brad looked up as if called upon in class without having done the homework. "That's a very good question. I was hoping you guys had some answers. That's really the point of my journey, to ask around and get a sense of what's happening."

John turned up the radio in order to better listen to Chrissie Hynde's heart-felt laments over the gentrification of her home state: "*Well, I went back to Ohio. But my family was gone. I stood on the back porch. There was nobody home.*"

Brad clued into the attention upon him being overshadowed by such a chestnut of pop culture. "You know, guys, it's all in that song. The powers that be can easily ruin it for the rest of us." He looked around and got nothing so he pressed on: "Hey, did you know that Rush Limbaugh stole the instrumental opening to this song to open his own show with? Yeah, he just up and took it without asking permission. It caused a big legal uproar between the record label and Limbaugh. Can you believe it?" Brad was on a jag and could hardly stop to catch his breath. "And the whole time that was going on, Chrissie Hynde was unaware of it. That was her song. She wrote it. Limbaugh stole it." He still wasn't getting the response he'd anticipated. Had they heard this story before? "Well, I just find what happened next to be utterly fascinating. It turns out that Limbaugh admired the guitar riffs but what he relished the most was using a liberal anthem in the service of his conservative cause!"

"It's a really great song," said Leslie, unsure of what to say.

"I know. I know. But, stay with me here, there's more. So, the legal battle is raging when Chrissie Hynde steps in and basically says, to hell with him, he can use the song. A licensing agreement was worked out with the payments being donated to PETA. Then, as an added twist, Limbaugh went above and beyond and came out in support of PETA. To this very day, he opens his show with that very same song!"

Maximo politely applauded. "What a great story!"

"Yeah, it seems everything you need to know about America can be found in that song. People can read into it whatever they like. You can enjoy it no matter what your politics. It's not meant to be an empty slogan and yet, by its easy-going accessibility it has been rendered sort of meaningless."

"That's going too far, don't you think?" pleaded Maximo.

"Oh, I don't know. Sometimes my commentary can have a little too much bite!"

They sat in silence and reverently listened to the rest of the song: *"The farms of Ohio had been replaced by shopping malls. And Muzak filled the air. From Seneca to Cuyahoga Falls. Said, ay, oh, way to go, Ohio."*

Finally, Brad looked up and asked the obvious question: "How far are you guys going?" To that, John shot back a direct response: "Just going as far as Columbus. That work for you?"

Brad looked appreciative for the relatively short trip. "Oh, that works for me!"

John, with a somewhat suspicious tone, asked, "So, where exactly are you from, Brad?"

Brad looked like a cornered animal. "Okay, I won't lie. I'm from Columbus!"

"Then this ride isn't really working for you, is it?" John demanded.

"I'm not perfect. I'm making this up as I go, just like your typical American, to be honest. We're all making it up as we go. We're all relying upon the same sound bites, the same slogans, the same lame lies. That's how we get someone so outrageously unreal into the White House. We're transfixed by the shadows on the wall. We don't know reality!"

John pulled the car over. They had reached Columbus. "Okay, that's cool. That's all good. So, no harm done in dropping you off here, Brad. You've had a productive day so far, lots to write about for your blog." John kept waving him off as Brad made his exit.

"Goodbye. Thank you for listening to what I had to say. I made no claim to have the answers!" With that last step out and his shutting the door, the car sped off.

"We could have been a little kinder to that blogger," said Maximo.

"No we couldn't," shot back John.

"He was pretty articulate," pleaded Maximo.

"He doesn't know anymore than we do. Actually, he appears to know less. And we're in pretty sorry shape. Our heads are full of talking points! All of us in our own perfect little bubble. How sad."

"John, just because you feel bad about yourself is no reason to dismiss him."

"Alright," said Leslie, "Brad did make a good point that we all rely upon pop culture more than we should. We all seem to know our pop culture better than just about anything else. Brad knows his factoids but he doesn't know about life."

"Yeah, he's just a Nowhere Man!" said Maximo. "You know, Mexicans love the Beatles so much. I think they might love the Beatles more than you guys here in the States!"

"Columbus doesn't look too bad for another gentrified wasteland. You've got a gig here and then we can aim for Philly, the City of Brotherly Love, by lunch time tomorrow. We'll be closing in on Charlottesville before you know it. Not too bad for a trio of out of touch elites." John let out a chuckle that fell to a low sigh.

"Yeah, Charlottesville is on the horizon," said Maximo, in a shaky tone, feeling a little anxious about it all.

"Well, sure. In the end, we get to Charlottesville and solve whatever mystery we can about your family history," pleaded Leslie.

"Don't get me wrong, that sounds good, that's the plan," sighed Maximo.

"Yeah, that's what I thought and…"started Leslie.

"Anyway," Maximo interrupted, "we're in the heart of Ohio. Is this the heart of Trump country or not?"

"Not exactly," said Leslie. "Maybe he won Ohio in the presidential election—but just barely."

"Way to go, Ohio."

Maximo performed the usual set of jokes he'd been working on. It didn't occur to him to try something different at the time. He was a bit worn out and the presence of John was something he was still getting used to. Later on, a light bulb went on above his head. He would have liked to have brought up Christopher Columbus in Columbus, Ohio.

# 31

When they reached Philadelphia, Maximo again asked, "Are we now in the land of Trump?" It was a great way to mark time and Maximo was genuinely curious. Leslie double-checked her facts on her phone. "No way. Trump won by a razor-thin margin here in 2016. You can't believe the hype from the Trump rallies."

They found the Mayfair Diner, a classic diner that had served as a campaign stop for Obama as well as served what sure tasted like authentic Philly cheesesteaks. Maximo was busy drawing something. "Hey there, buddy," John called out. "Your sub is going to get cold."

Leslie looked over at her twin lovers from across the table. She had one side all to herself and was engrossed in reading the latest news on her phone. "Wow, oh, wow," she began to get their attention. "Today, July 16, 2018, will go down in history as the day that Trump officially betrayed his country in favor of kissing Putin's ring at this press conference in Helsinki. I think I'm going to be sick. JFK would never have done this!"

It was truly a significant moment. Leslie took it to heart and took stock of where she was. She was a relatively young woman at 30. She was still searching. The whole transcript of the Helsinki press conference had just been made available and she carefully read it, preferring to do that before seeing the video. Trump had been in Europe for the annual NATO summit and had somehow created his own cozy summit for two by arranging this secretive meeting with Putin. There would be no transcript of the actual meeting.

At one point, Leslie couldn't help but gasp in recognition. It was bad enough that Trump had taken Putin's word for it when asked if Russia had meddled in the 2016 election. Trump trashed his own intelligence in favor of Putin. To add a touch of strange, Putin had his own personal response to special counsel Robert Mueller's request to question Russian officials. Putin suggested that a swap be made. Mueller could send some Americans to Russia for questioning. Among them, Putin was especially interested in businessman Bill Browder. Immediately, Leslie spotted a very specific lie. The only reason that Putin was interested in Browder was because Browder was a key player in exposing Putin's corruption. Putin didn't want to question Browder. Putin wanted Browder dead.

Putin and Trump both enjoyed telling lies and making threats right in the open, especially at a press conference being broadcast around the world. Leslie knew about Browder because she'd read his book, *Red Notice*. She bought the book at an airport bookstore and it struck her as a perfect window into the lawless world of Putin and the oligarchs. Russia has become toxic under Putin with corruption being the easy fix to whatever problem. When you have someone like Bill Browder get in the way, you get rid of him. That's exactly what happened to Browder's tax advisor Sergei Magnitsky. So, to have Putin outright lie that he was only interested in asking Browder a few questions was pretty nauseating.

This game of lying was something that defined both Trump and Putin. It was a blood sport that the two of them could not get enough of. For Trump, it was a game of counterpunching, always hit back harder. For Putin, it was similar, a duel to the death. The old Russian play of deceit was to take any accusation and turn it back around upon the opponent, accuse the accuser of the same thing but only worse. If you were being accused of robbing a bank, then the distraction was to accuse the accuser of robbery plus murder. Keep it simple and make it stick: "Fake News!" "Witch Hunt!"

"Guys, I'm telling you, today will be remembered as a very dark day, a day when the American president and the Russian president held a press conference to tell the world that everybody schemes so just get over it!" Leslie again studied her twin lovers. John gave her that quizzical look of his. Maximo looked back with a sense of acknowledgement.

"I get it, Leslie. We're being forced to accept the new normal. Hey, I don't like it one bit. And I think it's only going to get worse," said John.

"I agree with John. We're being asked to accept up is down and down is up. I think Trump is more than happy to conspire with Russians or whoever else gives him what he wants. But it's too much to even suggest that for some people," said Maximo, "I'm not going to say that JFK was perfect but, you're right, he would never have cozied up to the Russians the way Trump has."

"I like JFK's sad eyes. He was always thinking and growing and trying," said Leslie.

Maximo smiled at Leslie and then looked across their table at a vintage campaign poster for JFK. Atop ran the slogan, "A Time for Greatness."

# 32

When they reached Virginia, Maximo asked yet again, "Are we in Trump country?"

And Leslie snapped back, "No! Hillary won this state. And she won the popular vote across the country, don't forget! She won the popular vote by 3 million votes!"

"Okay, I believe you!" said Maximo, "I totally believe you. You're singing to the choir." The two of them laughed and giggled.

John, oh so firmly in the driver's seat, stared at his rearview to regard the cozy couple in the backseat. So, he'd let himself become the chauffer for these two! He couldn't help but make a snide remark: "Just look at West Virginia. Now, Max, there's your Trump country. He won that state hands down. They love him out there."

Maximo was awestruck and yelled out: "Then we must go!"

John was amused. Maybe this was exactly what Max needed, a nice shot of reality. So, without any interruption, John started driving right into Trump country. "Why do they love Trump so much over there?" asked Maximo.

John sighed: "He promised them something, salvation."

Maximo: "Salvation from what?"

John: "Anything that makes them sad."

Maximo: "Maybe I didn't pay much attention to what some people think makes them sad."

John kept on driving. Does Trump's base even go to comedy clubs? he wondered. Or is Maximo just going to pick a fight with the first good ole boy he finds? John decided to just keep driving and figure this out as they went along.

"Oh, I see now," muttered Maximo as he looked on Leslie's phone. "These people were promised they would keep working in the coal mines. What a horrible thing to promise! That is why they love him?"

Leslie chimed in: "Yeah, John, do you really think it's such a good idea for us to be going there?"

Maximo straightened up as if struck by an epiphany. "What a twisted thing to do. This corrupt playboy billionaire promises these down and out people that they get to continue working in the coal mines. Hey, as a very special gift from me to you, you get to keep working in the coal mines! Does it matter that this work is outdated? Does your health matter? Does the environment matter? Hell, no!"

Leslie could see a disaster in the making. "John, are you going to turn this car around or do I have to?"

"I must speak to these coal miners and let them know that they've all been sold a bill of goods. Coal is not the answer. It's a sick joke.

It's archaic technology. Trump is laughing at these people and they either don't know it or don't want to know it."

"John! Turn this car the fuck around!"

"Alright, I can't do this anymore," said John. He turned the car towards Virginia. "They will eat you for lunch, Max. I will admit, it's a suicide mission to go in there just looking for trouble."

Leslie turned her attention to Maximo. "You get that, don't you?"

Maximo sheepishly nodded. "You don't have to say another word."

"You really think these folks from God's country want to be lectured to about being duped by Donald Trump? And lectured to by a Mexican?" added John, his voice raised to a fine self-righteous tone. Maximo shrugged and looked away only to turn around again.

"You seem to forget you're every bit as much a Mexican as I am, John. You think you can float right through…and pass for white?"

"I'm not trying to float through anything. I'm not trying to pass for anything!"

"You ever call attention to your Mexican ancestry? It's not that far back. It's not far back at all. It goes back to your mother, John."

"Thanks for the history lesson, bro."

"It's not just history, bro. It's family. It's blood. You act as if blue blood runs through your veins, bro."

"Alright, you've had your say. Save some of that for your act."

"I'm just trying to figure things out, John."

"Yeah, alright. We're all just trying to figure things out. Good enough."

# 33

Everything had gone to a dark radio silence. Only the steady hum of the road barely registered. The sky was dark. John was but a dark figure behind the wheel. Maximo grew restless. "John, I hope you're looking forward to the next stop. It's going to be special." There was a slight, nearly imperceptible, nod and grunt from the driver's seat. "It's something that will wake us all up and refresh us."

"Maybe we've had enough surprises, Max."

"No, please listen. You must have a place in your heart for New York City!"

Again, John emitted a nearly inaudible grunt. Maximo waved a hand as if clearing a slate. "Let's do this right. We need to do this right. It's our next official tour stop. We're going to New York City!" John's head popped up and the car swerved for a second.

"Max, you're right! Yes, we're keeping to your schedule. New York City here we come! Woo hoo!"

The slight jolt from the car woke up Leslie, "Uh, what the fuck?"

John started to speed up to make up for his slow and steady driving. "Max here has got me pumped up. New York is the place to be. And New York will welcome him. New York loves people like Max!" He said this in such an upbeat and supportive way, as if he thought his shift in attitude was actually doing something good for Max. He didn't have to be told twice. John knew that, if there was one area of the country that was the best example of toughing out the worst and doing it with heart, it had to be New York City. If there was one area of the country that had heard it all but would still lend its ear, it had to be New York City.

"You're really excited about New York, huh?" asked Leslie, still unsure of what was happening.

"Max found my weakness. I can say, without hesitation, 'I love New York!'"

Maximo was pleased by how John and he could find common ground. They both loved New York! But were people programmed to be attracted to the Big Apple? Sure, there was some of that. The media had done its job well. But, at its core, the Big Apple was undeniably authentic. The bright lights/big city seemed to appeal to everyone for an unlimited amount reasons. Maximo was inclined to think that John and he were both attracted to some combination of the magical and wondrous. Both of them, he wanted to believe, were truly inspired by the massive accumulation of human struggle and achievement.

The next day, they drove right into the city. It was still well before rush hour and traffic was relatively reasonable. John, in an inspired mood, found a college buddy in Harlem who could put them up for the night. John even suggested a club where Maximo would have a good chance at getting to do an open mic, even though John had already been told that all the open mic dates had been prearranged by Jimmy Gold. Even the hotel stay had already been taken care but John would not take no for answer.

The three of them had settled into the apartment John had found for them and, having waited long enough, John made his big push for Maximo to be on his way. Maximo had just gotten back from walking Rico when John made his move. "Hey, it's starting to get on in the day. You don't want to miss your gig. Just hop on that subway and have a good time," said John, as if he were personally in charge, "And, once you're done, hop right back on that subway and meet us back here." John gave him a wide grin.

Maximo had no reason to feel at all grateful for John's sudden friendliness but offered a polite smile in return and asked, "You guys aren't going to be at the show?"

John shook his head. "Nope, I think we're all pretty tired, buddy. I think we plan to crash most of the time we're here. But you go out there and do your thing." How thoughtful of John! Yeah, the guy had a heart of gold. Maximo didn't see Leslie and assumed she was still napping. He really didn't have the time or the energy to argue with John. There was nothing left to do but leave.

Alright, he'd forget about everything for a little while. He couldn't just hop on a subway train from Frederick Douglas Circle. That was too easy. First, he'd cut through Central Park and soak up some authentic atmosphere, just like a native strolling down the avenue without a care in the world.

Unlike a tourist, Maximo took his time savoring very quiet moments by sitting at a park bench. An older couple sat right next to him. It was a man and woman, with the woman carrying most of the conversation. She proceeded to tell an old tale:

*"The story goes that you marry by the time you are twenty-one. If you don't, then you're going to be an old maid.*

*That's what she believed. So, the first guy who comes along, she marries. He was a broken-down looking man, nothing promising about him to look at him.*

*They decide upon running a business, a little shop. When they started out, he insisted on fixing the place up. One day, when she gets to the shop, she finds he's fixed up the windows with curtains but then she looks further. Inside, she finds that he's spread sanitary napkins on a table.*

*She goes over and tells that schmuck, 'Are you crazy? You sell sanitary napkins in boxes!'*

*He looks at her and he says, 'If you don't take them out of the boxes, then how are the customers supposed to know what's inside?'*

*Time passes. They move to Texas. He and his wife decided to buy some land. He has $1,500 and he collects another $1,500 from family. And so he gets himself some land. And it's a good investment since, as you'll see, it's close to something very important.*

*One day, an oil company asks to buy their land. But he won't sell it. Now, it was true that he wasn't cultured or good-looking but he was a shrewd businessman. He tells them that he'll lease his land and, if they should strike oil, then he gets a royalty.*

*Well, they did strike oil. And so, for the rest of his life, and his family to this day, have gotten royalties. Can you imagine?*

*He made millions, this schmuck who spread out sanitary napkins, and all from a $1,500 investment.*

*So, the moral to this story is to get married by age twenty-one. If it doesn't work out, you can always divorce him. But you can at least say you were once married."*

Maximo got up feeling quite refreshed after hearing such a story. There were all sorts, oh so many sorts, of stories to be told, to be overheard, and to be written down.

# 34

After a bit more wandering around, Maximo made it down to the Bowery and confirmed that he was on the open mic list. That part was easy. He still had some time to wander around so he made a pilgrimage of sorts. He walked right up to the last studio and home of Jean-Michel Basquiat. It was a ramshackle set of modest old buildings cobbled together. Nothing much to look at except that it had become nothing less than a shrine for both Andy Warhol and Jean-Michel Basquiat. The ghosts of both of these artists loomed large over New York City, especially in the Bowery. There had always been talk that Warhol used Basquiat or that Basquiat used Warhol. Who had exploited who? Wasn't it possible that these two misfits had found each other in the end and, for a little while, felt less lonely and more human as they worked together and became friends? The two buildings, dating back to before the Civil War, had housed some of Warhol's factory shenanigans. Basquiat had been renting out the spaces for his own use at the time of his death. In the years and decades to follow, the walls outside became covered in various tributes to both men.

Free from his mother's horrid domination, Maximo could stand before this Basquiat shrine and pay his respects. "I know that you suffered. I know that the art world, made up of rich powerful white people, was more than happy to devour its one black superstar. Would it be different today? It couldn't help but be different but would the progress be all that significant?" Maximo said this as if in a trance. He was simply speaking to a fellow artist, a fellow wounded artist now dead. "Just a few missteps, and it could have all been a different story for you. If you hadn't met their demands at any step of the way, who knows, maybe no one would ever have heard of you."

Maximo looked up at a big patch of brownstone and he could imagine Krazy Kat doing a little jig, one of these weird little dances from the comic strips followed by more loopy antics from the funny pages. What was Krazy Kat doing now? Who was Krazy Kat? What was Krazy Kat's true identity? Krazy Kat, the ultimate enigma! George Herriman, the ultimate enigma! Jean-Michel Basquiat, the ultimate enigma! No one likes being the Other. It drove Krazy Kat mad. It slowly killed Herriman. It quickly killed Basquiat. Basquiat braved through it as America's one and only renowned contemporary black artist. Herriman enjoyed the glory of success without the added distinction of being known as a great black artist. Instead, he chose to pass for white since it seemed to be his only option. And Krazy Kat, as a sort of alter ego to Herriman, belted out the cries of confusion and frustration only truly understood by someone who has been pegged as the Other. To label someone as the Other is a coward's delight, a way for that coward to feel superior. No one likes being the Other. It drove Krazy Kat mad. It slowly killed Herriman. It quickly killed Basquiat.

That night, Maximo went up on stage and delivered what he felt was a solid set. And, before he knew it, Maximo's fifteen minutes (or was it more like five minutes?) were up. It was time to recede back into the dark, into an audience made up mostly, or exclusively, of other aspiring comedians. Maximo hung around to catch as many acts as he could. Some were impressive and some were rough around the edges. And some of them, quite a lot of them, were highly confessional. Your typical emerging comic was not a truly self-aware writer, aware that it was more than alright to reveal a little and hide the rest. Many of these comics were broken and hurting. Lots of daddy issues. Lots of, all kinds of, issues. But Maximo was totally okay with whatever worked for a comic at a certain point in time. He wasn't judging anyone, just observing. He definitely knew he was hurting too. He was simply tuning into the humanity and artistry of comedy: an art form revolving around process, soul searching, and leaps of faith.

Maximo left the club feeling better for it. He'd learned a lot. The most important thing, regarding his act, was the fact that he was not alone. More often than he could have imagined, he heard comics talking about race. A lot of them were immigrants and they were less than at ease with the current political climate. A lot of them were Hispanic. And a lot of them were mixed race just like him. These comics spoke most eloquently when they let themselves be free to say they felt left out. One outsider after another, made the point clear: the world was cold enough as it was without people working hard to make it colder.

It was time for Maximo to get on a subway back to Harlem. He had really made quite an impression. It was as if being on stage was where he belonged all along but he couldn't see that until now. He'd allowed himself to hide and conform most of his life. There was still a chance to live the life he'd always been meant for.

# 35

When Maximo took the stage that night in a little Greenwich Village comedy club, it was the culmination of two things: all he'd learned so far about being in the States firsthand; and all he'd learned about comedy. The Lantern turned out to be a great club and Maximo was so proud to be there with his fellow comedians. It was a classic black box theater space, perfect for any performer at any level.

Maximo waited patiently and, when his name was called, he took the stage, as simple as that. It was as quick and as matter-of-fact an act as he could make it. The first rule of comedy, as Maximo saw it, was not to dwell on all the incidental stuff but save the lingering for bringing out the bit of comedy you're attempting. You don't even think about the fact you're out there attempting comedy; you go into a hyper-state of focus. It requires intelligence, confidence, and determination. And it has nothing to do with dumb luck.

There was still so much to learn. For now, Maximo had figured out a method that worked for him. He was constantly taking notes, rehearsing them in his head, and then refining his material. He didn't like to spend too much time looking at himself in the mirror and performing an act to himself. It sort of creeped him out, reminded him too much of Robert DeNiro in that movie where he plays a psycho comedian. There would be plenty of time for that kind of refinement, once he had material so pinned down that he was focusing on polishing it. Then again, he hoped to somehow avoid ever being too polished. Was that possible? In fact, he'd been editing material all along and he aimed for a very smooth delivery. As long as he didn't lose his natural delivery, then he was okay. Didn't people naturally think over what they wanted to say during a conversation? You could always tell if they were going in without much forethought or if they were heavily scripted. Anyway, he took the stage and did the latest version of his act:

"Hello, my name is Maximo Vijae. I am an illegal alien from Mexico." That line alone got the first laugh and a smattering of applause.

"I crossed the border in a hot air balloon." Laughs. Maximo paused for a beat in order to sustain it.

Maximo looked out at the audience. "Anyone else use a hot air balloon?" More laughs.

"I crash landed in San Diego. Nobody noticed. I had totally passed the border and landed somewhere in La Jolla" Someone yelled out an instant whoop of encouragement. "Okay, someone out there gets it."

"In fact, I was nearly naked when I reached the shore. Overall, I think I was doing okay even though I was in dire straits. I sometimes look my best when I'm in a panic. Well, just a little panic, like learning that my favorite show has been cancelled. I can give off that intriguing look of concern that only a Latin man can do." Maximo picked up on some soft low-key giggles followed by some loud clapping and hoots of approval.

"In Mexico, a regular guy like me can be a bit self-conscious about his body. In general, I'd say a lot of us are pretty modest whether we're average build or buff. But moving on to the bigger picture, to be honest, a concern for a lot of us men is getting pegged quickly as just the Mexican guy. What does that really mean anyway? I don't know. It can be the difference between being easily dismissed and being invited to the after party--or being asked if you want to join the wait staff at the after party. If your skin is light enough and your approach is light enough, then who knows what might happen. Suddenly, it's up for grabs. They just don't know. You might look to them as if you're French, Russian, Greek. Most people are ignorant enough that you can be whatever you tell them you are. Of course, you can really mess with them and just say you're Episcopalian and they probably won't question it and move on." A smattering of giggles followed, enough giggles to keep Maximo focused and confident.

"Of course, if you're supposed to be the Other, then who is the group that is supposed to be the Normal? For a very long time, that used to mean White Anglo-Saxon Protestant. It used to be a nuclear white family like the one on the '50s American sitcom, 'Leave it to Beaver.' That model makes no sense today. But Trump has dredged up some sort of return to the 'white silent majority.' That makes no sense today in a world that is more and more acknowledged and celebrated for its diversity, right? But Trump would have you believe that there are Others out there who need to be walled off and put in cages. How did we stumble back and step knee-deep into this bullshit? Well, that question won't be fully answered tonight. Lots of unpacking to do. Lots of work to do all around!" This inspires applause. People are really open to what Maximo is saying and it feels good. He let it soak in and stepped back a bit for some more easygoing laughs.

"You see a lot of things when you're on the road. There's supposedly a lot of these kitschy lame dinosaur statue roadside attractions out there but I didn't notice any of them. Maybe I wasn't paying attention. I probably just zoned them out. In Mexico, it takes a lot more than a dinosaur statue to get us excited. We're used to Aztec human sacrifices atop of pyramids, with pools of blood dripping down the steps. A little of that goes a long way."

"We haven't seen that kind of horror in a very long time. And then Trump comes up with human cages to house families seeking asylum. Now, that gets everybody's attention. Human cages?! You can't make that shit up!" Instant laugh, just as big or bigger than talking about a hot air balloon. "Some Trump staffer crunched the numbers and decided: 'You know what we need right about now? Human cages!' And so they went with that. Sure, we can get a whole bunch of human cages, enough to see us through to re-election. You've got this Trump base all stoked up with fear and hatred. They need their human cages!"

"Trump doesn't scare me and, at the same time, he is pretty scary. He's your basic bully. He likes to push on people. He likes to insult people. And he likes to strike fear into people. Wow, just what you want in a president of the United States, right?"

"Well, there are a number of things that trump a Trump. Truth, beauty, and the real American way. There's three to start with. I'll tell you, the one thing I love most about a road trip is getting back to nature. We have all these creature comforts for us humans, all these fatty snacks nicely packaged in plastic, all these coupons, and apps, and social media. Then, suddenly, you see an eagle swoop by. Or you see buffalo!"

"We all need a national day of awareness of the great outdoors. We need to be out in nature and see real colors again! We need to get naked, really primal, not just Paleo diet primal. We need to get naked and ride on the back of a mighty buffalo! Wouldn't that be something? It's not some sexual fantasy. No, I think we all have a real need to be out there in the wild as close to our animal roots as possible."

It was time to hold for a beat and take the pulse of the audience. Maximo tried to scan the audience despite the bright lights. It was a challenge to try to see beyond the stage. It was basically him balancing a bunch of things all at once: his posture, his timing, and his voice carrying nicely over the microphone. "Anyone out there wish they were naked riding on the back of a buffalo?" Someone yelled out a whoop. "Alright, then, I knew I wasn't the only one! And, with that, I thank you all for your time!"

# 36

The next day, it was time to turn things back on course to Virginia. It would be a long hard drive but John was up for it.

The three of them seemed to be in good spirits. "A quick bite out of the Big Apple will do wonders for you, huh, Max?" John threw that out with no expectation of any clever response.

Max momentarily straightened up a bit, as if ready to explain himself, but suddenly let himself sink back down. "Yeah, it will work wonders." Actually, he would have loved an explanation of how John and Leslie had spent their time together alone but he wasn't going to do that.

"I can offer another bit of goodwill towards you, buddy. I think we've earned ourselves a visit to our nation's capitol, Washington, D.C.!"

Maximo immediately perked up. "That's great that you're excited about that since it is one of our tour dates, in fact, it's our last official stop."

"Well, then it's meant to be. I was messing around on my phone and I easily found a friend who will put us up for the night in Georgetown. It'll be really nice."

Leslie let out with a cheerful: "Whoop! Whoop! Whoop!"

"Alrighty then, sounds like it's settled," John said with a cocky tone. He was in charge. He was calling the shots. And he was in control of bestowing gifts. John, the oh so generous gift-giver.

"Thank you, John," Maximo said without hesitation, "We are grateful. We did have a hotel already arranged but your offer is nice so thank you. We accept."

John made a show of raising his shoulders in a mock shrug: "Ah, it's just what I do!"

By the time they reached the D.C. metro area, it was pretty backed up with traffic. John was a bit less joyful and more focused on finding their destination. Eventually, they located the brownstone on a narrow street right in the thick of all the tony and gentrified surroundings. It was definitely worth the effort. John's friend, Paul, was very kind and gracious. He couldn't hang out with them for long as he had a date that evening. All things considered, he suggested they might enjoy a walk that led down to some nice shops and restaurants. Paul was sensitive to the JFK references that Maximo made and he specifically suggested that they go visit Martin's Tavern, a favorite haunt of John F. Kennedy throughout his political career.

When they arrived at Martin's Tavern, they were greeted by the manager who immediately began a scripted introduction: "Over there is the JFK rumble seat booth where JFK preferred to have his breakfast. Next to that is a booth preferred by Richard Nixon, who happened to be a friendly rival of JFK. And next to that booth is where JFK proposed to Jackie." Maximo's eyes widened as he took it all in.

"Would it be alright if we sat in the booth where JFK proposed to Jackie?" asked Maximo. "Why, of course," replied the manager, "you are most welcome to that booth." He directed the three and then took a moment to observe John and Maximo. "I must say, you gentlemen both have Kennedy features. Are you, by chance, related to the family?" John let out a muffled scoff. Maximo gave an enigmatic smile before saying: "That, my friend, is quite a question. It is, indeed, a possibility."

Once the manager left, John took a long look at Maximo. "I never know what to tell people and I should have developed a pretty solid stock response by now. Someone named, John F. Kennedy, who has that Kennedy look, should really have a ready line or two. But I don't."

Maximo placed his hands flat on the worn wooden table. "Say what you will about John Kennedy but he is a giant among so many ants that scramble around today."

John sniffed the air. "You get no argument out of me, brother."

"Can you sense greatness in the air?"

John sighed, "Please, I don't want to argue. I love Camelot as much as the next guy."

"Camelot!"


"I'll have the clam chowder. Don't you think that was one of his favorites? Yeah, I could see Jack with a steaming cup of good ole chowder."

"You're ruining the mood, John."

"I'm sorry."

They decided that one tourist trap was not nearly enough for them so they took a cab down to the National Mall. "When was the last time we were in D.C., John? It was years ago. You had a conference. It was a brief visit, as I recall. We had time to just take in a few hot spots, more or less like right now." Leslie and John regarded each other and then redirected their gaze down to Capitol Hill. The three strolled within the campus of Smithsonian museums. "I've always meant to go to the Hishhorn. Don't tell me we're too late." Leslie looked at John with mock desperation. "Alright, I won't tell you but, in fact, we are too late."

It was too late to go to any museums. "I know what we can still do. Once it gets dark, it's a treat to see all the monuments lit up, right?" Leslie asked, not at all sure of the answer. John shrugged. "We can at least go see the White House right now." Leslie turned to Maximo, "You would like that, wouldn't you, Max?" He thought it over and it seemed to him that more of Georgetown would have rounded out the night very nicely. "Okay, that sounds fine."

The White House, from the north, provided the public with a relatively close view of the venerable structure. You couldn't get right up to the fence but close enough. The actual lawn seemed fairly modest as far as mansions were concerned. Maximo was intrigued with viewing the iconic home of presidents, seeing it in person, at a human scale. "Somehow, I pictured it being bigger. Seeing it in context like this, it looks so finite, so vulnerable. It can only be what it is, no more, no less." John had to chime in. "It's no Buckingham Palace, that's for sure. But that's because we Americans elect a president. We don't have a king or queen presiding over us, now do we?"

Maximo had little energy left to engage with John and simply let himself recede into the background. John and Leslie began to casually banter and nonchalantly made note of Maximo wandering over to take in the whole scene. A open lane separated the White House from Lafayette Park. It was from the lane onward to the park that a variety of protesters took root, some with their own makeshift booths. On that day, the prominent protester was a man wearing a colorful robe with a pattern made up of donkeys and elephants, goggles, along with a golden top hat and shiny boots. He was the self-proclaimed, Political Wizard. He certainly looked the part, complete with Santa Clause white beard and long hair. Maximo couldn't help but approach him. The strange wizard immediately came to life: "Hello, are you hear in support of or in protest of Donald Trump?" Maximo hesitated, wondering if it was a trick question. "I'm looking for peace and understanding," began Maximo.

"Peace and understanding? Do you realize where you are? This place is just the opposite!" Maximo was encouraged by this remark. Perhaps the wizard was on the same page with him.

"Do you mean to say that you are neither for nor against the current president?" The wizard was an insistent sort. Maximo shrugged and finally confided his bias, if that was really what it was. "You could say that I'm against Donald Trump."

"You could say that? But I'm asking you. Don't you know your own mind? Don't you know what you're saying?" Alright then, the wizard was right. Wasn't that what Maximo had been saying all along during his comedy tour? "Yes, wizard! I am saying that I do not support Trump!"

"Much better! We must say what we mean and mean what we say!"

Maximo turned around to share this remarkable wizard with John and Leslie. He walked over and finally got their attention. But, when he returned, the wizard was gone.

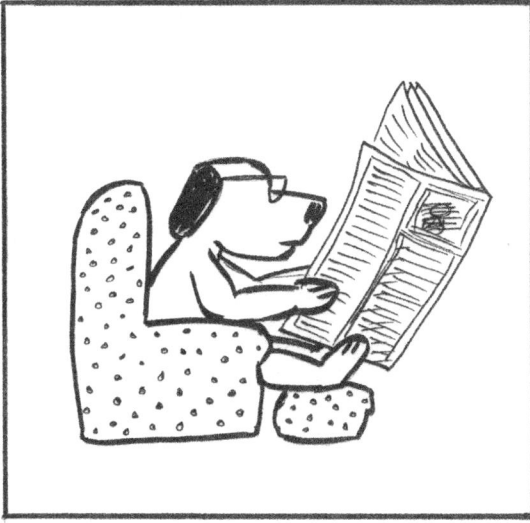

# 37

It was hard to leave Washington D.C. right away. The trio couldn't help but linger and ended up spending a good part of the next day wandering some more.

They had one last meal, lunch at Old Ebbitt Grill, a landmark restaurant favored by diplomats and lobbyists alike. The tables were close together and quite busy. They felt lucky to be seated as soon as they were.

"Everywhere we go, there are placards, statues, all kinds of reminders of the Civil War," said Maximo. "It is the American Civil War that still hangs heavy over the capitol. It doesn't need the likes of Donald Trump to kick up old resentments and tear open old wounds."

An older couple, a distinguished looking man and woman, were listening intently. The man cut in: "Young man, as long as there's blood-soaked earth, the Civil War lives on."

Uh oh. Maximo really didn't want to step into something. He had been eager to pick a fight only days before but, right at that moment, he preferred to tread lightly.

"I'm sure that the Civil War is far from forgotten," offered Maximo as a compromise.

"Forgotten? Never!"

Maximo began to reconsider his options. This could easily become ugly. Did he want to break into his own version of the Rock Hudson diner scene at this antique of a restaurant? Was he ready to rumble with a senior citizen? But then it happened and perhaps it was inevitable.

"You Mexican, son?" asked the old man.

"Excuse me?" Maximo could feel the temperature suddenly shoot up, alarm bells ringing throughout his very being. It made him dizzy angry.

"Mexicans. Now, that's one hell of mess. You people are taking jobs away from honest hard-working Americans. You're lazy and hurting people too. You should go back where you came from, wetback."

"You need to cool your jets right now, granpa. I'm not going to tolerate your ignorant hatred on my last day in the capitol. You persist in spewing out that chickenshit and I will take that prime rib and shove it up your ass. Are we clear?"

The old man's jaw dropped and his false teeth popped out. He slumped in his chair, utterly deflated. He looked like he'd lost three shades of color. He looked away, raised a trembling hand waving off any further exchange. He was surrendering before dessert was served. The South would not be rising again that day.

Maximo felt terrible but also quite relieved. The old man had become as quiet and docile as a little lamb. Maximo looked back at

138

John and Leslie. "Hey, sometimes you gotta do what you gotta do. Say what you mean and mean what you say!"

Finally, they went on their way. By nightfall, they were in Charlottesville. It reminded Maximo a little bit of Georgetown: old, quiet, rarefied—or was that basically an all around uptight vibe? Everything around him had a finely manicured look as if Martha Stewart had run around dusting and scrubbing every nook and cranny. He sensed that it was yet another place where you could easily shut yourself off from the rest of the world. People might be very polite, very civil and genteel, while also hiding their true selves. But then that tragic event happened here not so long ago. It happened so suddenly as it ripped its way through. Everything laid bare, out into the open. A great national dysfunction exposed for all to see around the globe. Nothing was spared. The cloak of secrecy, the collective veil of denial, yanked away.

They arrived much later than they anticipated but still eager to work off nervous energy. "John, would you drive over to where it happened?" Leslie asked with such a somber voice that he couldn't resist. He knew exactly where she meant. All he had to do was look at his phone and he'd find it.

They got out of the car and walked around. It was dark and quiet. None of them had a word to say. They all stopped abruptly at the foot of the statue of Robert E. Lee. It was a handsome statue, as far as statues went. But it was tainted goods. It was debatable as to what it was honoring as it did not originate in the aftermath of the American Civil War. In fact, it was not erected until 1924, quite a long delay for erecting a Civil War monument. But quite in tune with the surge of support for white supremacy at the time.

On August 11, 2017, white nationalists marched in protest of the city's plans to remove the statue of Robert E. Lee. Activists were there in opposition. A fight broke out and a white supremacist mowed his car into the counter-protesters, killing activist Heather D. Heyer. The next day, Trump blamed both sides and, a few days later, reiterated that claim. It was a calculated move to placate segments of his political base. As far as Trump was concerned, there was nothing wrong with declaring a moral equivalency between the neo-Nazis and the counter-protesters.

It was dark and quiet. No one said a word. They found a hotel in the middle of town. The front desk agent was an upbeat young man. "Y'all here got a kid going to UVA?"

No one felt like much small talk but John chimed in, "Nope. Just passing through."

The clerk could not leave well enough alone. "You are right next to the University of Virginia, as you know. Beautiful campus. You're not too far from Monticello, of course."

John slapped his forehead. "Wait, are you telling me we're in Virginia? Charlottesville? You know what we're also not too far from? That atrocious statue of Robert E. Lee!" The clerk just froze and the blood seemed to drain from his complexion leaving him with the palest shade of white. Maximo took charge long enough to make sure that everyone had their own separate hotel room. He made sure to pay for that himself. Then everyone marched to their respective room and promptly went to sleep. It was just a matter of some old-fashioned sleuthing that lay ahead for them the next day.

# 38

It was finally the morning before the big day. Maximo got up and went to what had become his familiar on-the-road perch consisting of writing desk, coffee and leather bound journal. This morning he had one last go at collecting his thoughts before another major event. Today he would plunge into learning more than ever about his past. Those old musty records would reveal something for sure but, then again, he had that journal staring him right in the face. There was still plenty of soil to till there. Another pair of stuck pages, another gentle peeling back, another drawing revealed, something more from ancient Mesoamerica. It was a beautifully rendered figure in full regalia with the title underneath, "Huitzilopochtli." A quick internet search revealed this to be the father figure god of the Aztec. He looked every part the patriarch, the wise leader.

Time was getting the better of him. He ploughed through some more, just to see what he might land upon. He settled his eyes on a random entry:

*Looks like Robbie and me got to go camping after all. He's the strong and silent type and not particularly friendly. We had fallen into a friendship of convenience. He was my guide who could speak fluent Spanish. And I was the man who provided the car for our excursions. We'd set out to see as much as possible on prescribed dates and times. And then, out of the blue, Robbie volunteered the idea that we go on a hike, just for the hell of it. Just the two of us, we were sleeping out amid the starry night. I was caught by surprise, a pleasant surprise. I think it was a genuine act of kindness, maybe pity, if not a real sign of friendship. Having a true friend in the world, well, that could be asking for too much. At least I got to share a night under the stars with a temporary friend.*

Maximo gently set the book down. In that moment, he could feel his father's suffering. "I'm sorry if you were lonely." Just then, there was a knock at the door, three quick raps, as if an urgent signal.

Leslie was at his door. He let her in, tempted to give her a hug but also very concerned at her risking a confrontation with John. "Hey, good morning. But what the hell are you doing?" Maximo said it in a playful and ironic way that he knew Leslie would get right away. And she did get it right away too. How grateful he was for small favors.

"Don't worry. I said I just needed to go out for a quick run. And then I promptly ran over here to see you!" Again, this triggered an overwhelming heartbreaking urge to hug her but he resisted.

"Look, I think we've got a lot to figure out."

"I'm not going to open a big can of worms. I just wanted to say hello. And, I guess, I wanted to just say…" What did she want to say? She looked at Maximo for the maximum amount of time allowed to better frame her thoughts. "Alright, I don't want you knocking yourself out on stage trying to prove anything to anyone. I'm so happy with you just the way you are."

"I know. I'm trying to be as authentic as I can possibly be."

"Yeah, yeah. I don't want you to feel obligated to put on an act that helps to explain, or justify, who you are. You don't have to be this ideal example of the Mexican people. You don't have to be a Mexican version of Sidney Poitier!" That instantly got Maximo's attention. "Sidney Poitier? The duke of cool, very articulate and immaculate." Maximo gave out a deep sigh. "Well, I think that kind of armor helps a lot of people get through their lives, including my own."

Maximo knew exactly what Leslie was getting at. He did feel that he was fighting an image, an image that was meant to belittle him, make him feel shame. "You know when Trump talks about The Wall and when he talks about caravans filled to the brim with drug smugglers and rapists, all of that shit. It's not only meant to gin up his bigoted base of support but it's meant to keep people off balance and make them afraid and feel powerless. That strategy wants people like me to be afraid and wish we didn't even exist."

This time an urge to hug got the better of Leslie. She pushed hard onto his chest and held him tight, rocking back and forth for the longest time. If only they could remain alone and quiet long enough to really figure it all out.

Maximo, still holding tight, went on: "When you get right down to it, I'm a citizen of the world. We all are. We're human beings. We're not nationalists; that's just crazy. I'm a goofy couch potato geek. I also happen to be Mexican. I happen to be a lot of things. And I'll tell you what, the sooner we can acknowledge that we're all just a bunch of humans…"

Leslie got closer, thought she might kiss him, but he turned away, turned his back to her. Was he sobbing? She pulled in close, leaned in and rested her body behind him. "I'm sorry, Maximo. I'm so sorry."

# 39

Williams & Williams was a grand ole law firm. It was both grandiose and modest in comparison to many a contemporary mid-sized firm. There was a lot of hard won tradition and history on display. But it was also in need of some refurbishing. And it smelled of a fine mist of tobacco, scotch and dirty socks.

It didn't take too long to see that they might have an uphill climb on their hands. They didn't exactly have all that much in the way of information to help move their investigation forward. Here are two men who are twins who would like to know about their long-lost father but they don't even know his name.

The JFK connection. Yes, that was the most distinctive of birthdates. Had they considered calling upon the local hospitals? asked the clerk. They were so lucky to be received by a friendly and kind face at the front desk. But there was only so much that could be done with so little to work with.

The trio was just about to walk out when they heard an older man call out.

"You there, I say, please come back. I heard that you're the twins that were born on the day that President Kennedy was assassinated!"

Leslie, John, and Maximo turned around. They took a good long hard look. The man was old enough to be John and Maximo's father. There was a look in his face, something instantly familiar about him. "You there, come here. You two boys, come here now!"

Maximo reached the old man first. "Sir, are you who I think you are? Were you in Mexico City? Did you and my mother…"

John walked at a tentative pace. He had made an ass of himself in the past, that was clear, but he'd gotten a chance redeem himself and made some progress. He'd made an effort to make it up to Maximo and, especially, to Leslie. In his heart, he really didn't care about the mystery of his father. He walked even slower. *Let Maximo take it in. Let Maximo have his moment. That's his father staring him in the face. Can't he see it by now? That crazy fuck is still wondering! I should go right up and introduce them to each other!*

Before Maximo could say another word, the old man raised a hand and gently placed it upon Maximo's forehead. "Come here, son. It's alright. I've been absent from you all your life but I'm here now. Can you accept that?"

The man had remained seated. Maximo was so overcome that he fell to his knees. He put his arms around the man. "I don't know a thing about you. But I love you!"

Leslie and John witnessed the scene from afar. Leslie kept Rico securely in her bag lest he run off and, out of instinct, maybe bite the mysterious old man. She looked over at John and slid her hand into his. She let it linger and let the warmth take hold. John was startled and immediately humbled. "I don't deserve this. I'm not worthy. When it's all said and done, I'm just not worthy." Sure, they'd gotten a little closer that day in New York. It was just a nice pleasant day together. But, then again, when was the last time they'd had that? It felt as if they had connected that day. And now he was genuinely hesitating and that only made him more attractive to Leslie.

"Hush, I know you're in as much turmoil as Maximo. You think you're so strong. Let's all three stick together and see how that fits."

John was beyond surprised. "Now, what exactly did you have in mind?"

"I don't know yet," answered Leslie, "but in these strange times, I think we need every friend we can get! I really don't know. But I don't think we should all just split up and go our separate ways."

# 40

Cecil cleared his throat. Maximo regarded him with equal amounts of love and curiosity. He was 88 years-old and looked like what he might imagine his father to look like, if that made any sense. Cecil gently placed a hand on Maximo's arm. "Listen, my son, I want to tell you a story."

It was back in the summer of 1962 that Cecil Kennedy struck out for Mexico. He was 32 years-old and felt like he was little more than a lost babe in the woods. His family was indirectly financing his latest adventure. They kept helping him out, or "bailing him out," as his father liked to say. But he knew how to earn a living. He'd been in the army. He'd been a school teacher. He just needed a little more time, things were still not adding up for him. What he really wanted to be was a writer. His prose paled in comparison to the power of William Faulkner and he was painfully aware of that. But, given a chance, his prose might at least rise to the level of another of his literary heroes, the overly sentimental yet oddly compelling Thomas Wolfe.

Cecil just needed a little more time, that was all. He could wait on his literary ambitions. But his loins, now that was another matter. He'd been through one sweet and innocent courtship after another with nothing that, how should he put it, nothing that bared any fruit. He needed to turn his life around soon. He looked in the mirror and he fancied himself a competent and handsome man but far too innocent for his own good.

It was on a day that he set out to see the Aztec pyramids, or was it the Mayan ruins, that he first met Maria. And it would be Maria who singlehandedly turned his life around. In retrospect, she hardly got the credit she deserved for the impact she made on him. Cecil was like so many Americans: take and take and take and then forget where you took it from. One's very survival can be thanks to one enchanting Mexican woman and then suddenly she can be virtually forgotten.

The original plan had been for Cecil to go to school in Mexico City and study creative writing. With a little bit of luck, he could live frugally and take his time developing his craft. That plan was still in place when Maria crossed his path and it remained in place for as long as he could sustain it. But, once their destinies collided, fate had a way of stepping in. It had been such a beautiful day. Cecil had a friend, Joe, who served as a guide and spoke fluent Spanish. Cecil provided the car. They drove in the direction of adventure. Joe began to mention that he'd read that somewhere out in the desert, just outside of the sleepy town of Texcoco, there was a site that held a huge stone head. It was known as, Tlaloc. If they could track it down, fame and fortune awaited them. The new museum of anthropology, recently built in Mexico City, would gladly pay them for their troubles if they should retrieve it. All they needed to do was ask around for directions since they barely knew where they were going.

Luckily, they happened upon what seemed like a very pleasant and inviting colonia neighborhood. And they happened to drive up just as someone was peeking out from a window to a walled off residence. Indeed, they were in luck. Maria, a pretty young woman, stepped out and convinced the two men that she knew where to find the infamous Tlaloc ancient ruin. They spent the rest of the day literally driving in circles. Maria found Cecil to be the dashing North

American she'd always dreamt of. The man who might make it possible for her to finally leave her family's home. And Cecil was overcome with the intoxicating attention he received from Maria. His writing ambitions would have to take a backseat in favor of his new romance. By the end of that first day, it didn't matter that Maria had lied to him about knowing anything having to do with Tlaloc.

A whirlwind romance ensued to put it mildly. Cecil and Maria were utterly inseparable. While it was unheard of for a young woman like Maria to engage in sex before marriage, the constant heavy petting between them got the better of the two love birds. And, once that virginal barrier had been broken, they couldn't possibly keep their hands off each other. It should not have come as a shock when Maria became pregnant but shocked she was all the same, more like terrified. This new development occurred after one of the love birds had flown the coop. Cecil had already returned to the United States.

As the relationship had continued to grow, Cecil felt that he wasn't as committed as he thought he was. It seemed to him that the best thing to do was simply to break up. It was only many months later that he learned he would soon become a father. He returned to Mexico a few days before the birth. And then that diabolic day unfolded. Cecil was to witness the birth of his twin boys just as news broke of the assassination. It spun his head like a cyclone.

How was it possible that his boys were born on such a date, at precisely that time? Cecil couldn't help but keep asking that question. Maria acknowledged it was a tragedy but she couldn't understand why Cecil was so transfixed by it. After all, he was a father now. He needed to be grounded for the sake of his new family. But that tragic day was to take its toll directly on Maria. After months of waffling over what he was to do next, Cecil decided it was best if he returned to the United States. He concluded that they needed to go back to their original arrangement of separate lives. He honestly did not see a life ahead of himself with Maria as his wife.

Such thinking was beyond belief for Maria but Cecil was determined and suddenly set a plan in motion with rapid speed. Before Maria was able to take it all in, she'd agreed to Cecil leaving with one of the boys. As a way of compensation, he'd made arrangements for her and her son to be looked after through one of his family's business ventures. The details were murky at best and made as much sense as saying the moon was made of green cheese but Maria accepted. She accepted; she'd made a choice. Cecil could always go back to that when he started to feel pangs of guilt. This way, he rationalized, she got her independence from her domineering family. It was a partial victory, wasn't it? It was a partial Cinderella happy ending, minus the handsome prince.

To think, all of this could be traced back to searching for the great ancient head of Tlaloc. What if they'd found it? Perhaps they did in a sense. Tlaloc, the god of rain, lightning and thunder--and fertility--seemed to have found them.

# 41

And so a story emerged that made sense to Maximo. It was the old man, Cecil Kennedy, who had made that fateful trip to Mexico. It was to be the adventure of a lifetime. He had plans that included exploring the Aztec pyramids, becoming a writer and perhaps bedding a cute native. Then he met Maria. Later, he broke up with her and, for a time, became a salesman. He was eager back then to make a go of setting up workshops that followed the guidelines laid out by self-help guru Dale Carnegie, author of the celebrated, "How to Win Friends and Influence People." And, for a very brief time, he indulged the notion that maybe he could do well both in the U.S. and in Mexico as a Dale Carnegie disciple.

Okay, so that explained all the quaint sayings in that old leather bound notebook. Those were all upbeat affirmations attached to Dale Carnegie. If there was anything else to it, well, that could be a story for another time.

Cecil's plans didn't exactly pan out. He did get to explore the Aztec pyramids. And he did start up a romance with a pretty local girl. But was he really going to make his fortune persuading people to improve their public speaking? After a long while of back and forth delaying, our man got cold feet in more ways than one.

It was that fateful day that changed everything. For some dark and inexplicable reason, his twin sons were born at precisely the time of the Kennedy assassination. Maximo had been born exactly on the dot. John, only moments later. What it meant, if anything, was beyond poor Cecil's reasoning. He wasn't related to the famous Kennedy family either, or so he claimed.

In the panic and chaos of the crisis atmosphere, and with a dire need to break his fate, Cecil made a most extreme decision. He would leave Maximo with Maria and he would return with John. But, even with one son, he felt the burden would be too much for him. He put John up for adoption, through a special venue. Cecil wasn't without a few connections. He knew of a wealthy colleague who had always wanted a son. In due time, Cecil went to law school and became a partner with Williams & Williams.

And so Maximo had some answers. They weren't exactly the answers he had hoped for but at least he had something. He didn't hate Cecil for it either. Cecil was less than courageous but he didn't hate him.

He would need time to process this further. Only now did the notes in the leather bound book start to take on greater meaning for him. The one quote that stood out from all the others was one Dale Carnegie lifted from Abraham Lincoln. In the aftermath of the Civil War, when resentment of the South seemed impossible to quell, Lincoln said this: "Don't criticize them: they are just what we would be under similar circumstances." Nothing could be more true or relevant to today's political climate. Were those who did not support Trump obligated to be civil to those Trump supporters who reveled in being unciv

**42**

Maximo found himself, seemingly overnight, with a budding career in stand-up comedy. "I'll take it!" was Maximo's joyful response to an offer of representation. He now had an agent that would look out for him, as well as Leslie if she was interested. Jimmy Gold had operated a hands-off approach the whole time but the New York City gig was special so he made sure to have an assistant take in the show and report back to him.

Something had happened that night he did his gig in New York. There was electricity in the air. He was as if under a spell. He looked back on it and he recalled his smooth delivery: every word right in the moment, every beat perfectly timed. He was making love to his audience. And who knows, for sure, who was in the audience, just how many people he had reached. People in the United States, he observed, could turn on you if they sensed you weren't sophisticated enough or if they sensed you were too sophisticated! It made no sense but taking an extreme view never did. It seemed that the solution was to strike the right balance, somehow transcend the popular consensus and that's exactly what he'd managed to do. He was feeding off everyone's energy that night and he could feel he'd done good. He spoke in a common language that everyone could understand. And, sure, not everyone was going to agree with him every time but he felt that he'd gained their attention and their respect.

And there was a new call from the home office. Just to clear up matters, Maximo was owed some money after all. It turned out that his mother did carry over her eye for detail when it came to his future. She had saved up a tidy sum and that, along with some other assets, would secure Maximo's future. He could easily do as he pleased. Maximo was on the most secure footing he'd ever known. He had a lot of structure now and a well-defined career was his for the taking. What would he do next with this opportunity? It looked like he was heading in the right direction but there is always the risk of going off course. He'd try to be extra careful.

The Williams & Williams firm had some good news too. Just in case it went unnoticed, there was nothing illegal about Maximo being in the United States. Since it was established that his father was a U.S. citizen, that meant that Maximo had dual citizenship. He was as much a citizen of Mexico as he was a U.S. citizen. Well, the likes of Trump would just have to take it and lump it. Maximo was here to stay!

"It makes complete sense that I have a dual citizenship. I am literally from two different worlds! Odd how I've felt like an outsider in both worlds! Odd how people from both of these worlds are so separated."

"Maximo, didn't you hear? Trump is trying to build this great big wall and, get this, he's going to get Mexico to pay for it!" said Leslie with more than just a pinch of irony.

"I know. We've all had to hear this cheap talk for so long. The U.S. needs stronger border protection to keep all the evil Mexicans out. The Mexicans are demons and don't deserve to be thought of as human beings. They should be caged. They should be treated as animals, even worse than animals."

"You don't separate mothers from their children. Not unless you're Donald Trump."

"Think of all the material I have to work with on stage, Leslie. It never ends with Trump or what comes after that. But let's hope for the best."

"The age of Trump will end and we won't miss it one bit."

## 43

Was this the end of Maximo's story? Well, it very well could be just the beginning. Trump, just like anything else, would eventually fade away. But a Trump legacy, whatever that was, would stink things up long after a Trump departure. America would need time to rebuild and repair and it was always in need of a good hero and a good laugh. Whatever was to happen next, it looked like Maximo had a very promising future ahead of him.

Maximo was lured into taking the long road trip back to Seattle. Leslie made the case that Maximo still needed a home base and, besides that, she wasn't ready to give him up. She managed to corner him for a brief but significant moment. John was at loose ends as to how they would proceed. He excused himself for a few minutes. The three of them were in a coffee shop. Maximo's luggage was still in the trunk of the car. "Where the hell are you supposed to go right now?" pleaded Leslie. Maximo shrugged.

"I've been told that I'm not from around here. I've had enough people across the country make that clear to me. And I am trying to make it clear to them that they've got it wrong. I am from around here!" Maximo began to pace a little and then stopped. "A lot of people already agree, already know, that I'm from around here!"

"I know, baby! You need your strength. You need support, emotional support. I still want to help you. I want you to get your voice out there."

"When I'm on stage, I feel that I'm there for a purpose. I have a purpose. I'm connecting with people. I'm making a difference."

"You can keep doing that. And I can help. Everybody can use a helping hand. I haven't forgotten about us. It wasn't that long ago that we made love, Maximo. It's been a whirlwind of activity. You. Me. John. Rinse. Repeat. But you've got something very special going on. I want to be a part of it."

"I know. I know. But what about John?"

"You can just leave it up to me. I'll play John like a fiddle."

"You don't have to play me like anything!" said John as he crept up on Leslie. And then he chuckled. It was a light-hearted chuckle, no anger, just a sort of sad and tired acceptance of his fate. "Hey, man, whatever happens happens!" Leslie had the upper hand. "Yep, that's how the whole country feels!"

John motioned for everyone to follow him. They had a new journey ahead of them. "The America I grew up with has been hijacked by a hatemonger. I want to live to see the repair work up ahead. And so my main goal, as far as I'm concerned, is to stay sane and healthy. We can't lower the bar much lower than it is now but I'm patient. I can wait out anything. Alright, let's get out of here!"

John was working from some renewed sense of purpose of his own. He'd witnessed firsthand how shabbily Maximo had been treated. What happened to Max could just as easily have happened to him. They were identical twins but somehow Max had been taking a beating while John got to sit back. Had he been lulled into a false sense of security from his upbringing? While he did enjoy berating Max for having been out of touch, living in a bubble, wasn't he just as guilty of doing the same thing? As long as neither one of them called attention to themselves and kept to their dull routines, no harm would come to them. But the moment either one of them stepped out of line, struck out on their own, spoke their mind, there would be consequences.

The car drove off at a respectful speed. Maximo and Leslie had somehow managed to sit in the backseat. They had fallen asleep together. That left John as the sad sack chauffer. Or maybe he had to shake off that kind of thinking once and for all. Just then, he was overwhelmed with a feeling of gratitude that he was, at least, safe and alive. *I want to feel more than that*, John brooded. *I'm so done with all these small consolations. I'm so done with the Orwellian chant of making America great again. I'll keep my eye on the road. I'll keep my eye of the horizon. The American dream is not some cheap slogan. For now, I'll just keep driving.*

# Epilogue

There are any number of fitting bits of closing evidence that the Trump era will be a perpetually cringe-worthy experience to remember. All the signs have been there going back to the very beginning of the Trump regime and even decades prior. All the signs of corruption, incompetence, and even collusion, all before the release of any official final report. How about Trump's endless contradictory statements or outright lies? Well, there are simply so many to choose from.

While it would seem to be a ridiculously futile endeavor to create a presidential library to the Trump era, perhaps it may play a useful role as a Museum of Lies. Such a place could be dedicated to the serious study of deceit. There could even be a special Kellyanne Conway wing devoted to Alternative Facts. There could be a screen welcoming visitors that could display a video loop of the exchange between Kellyanne Conway, counselor to the President, and Chuck Todd, moderator of NBC's *Meet the Press*, during an interview on January 22, 2017, in which she defended White House Press

Secretary Sean Spicer's false statement about the attendance numbers to Trump's inauguration as President of the United States.

It may sound farfetched, or partisan, to suggest a Trump library would be nothing more than a Museum of Lies. It may sound downright silly but what would a Trump presidential library end up being but a repository for the spinning of history at a level never before imagined? A Trump library might serve a useful purpose but only if it evolved into a serious study of deceit, which it may very well inevitably have no choice but to do.

Numerous commentators have gone to great lengths to state that the level of deceit coming from the Trump era is probably something not known in recent memory, or the modern era. But that is an incredibly mild assessment. The level of Trump deceit, it is safe to say, is on a level all its own, led by the incomparable Trump himself. And another thing to always keep in mind: what Trump has gotten away with is equal to the overall complacency of all of those who could have acted, along the way, to remove him from office or to have kept him from gaining office in the first place.

In closing, among the treasure trove of all things Trump, here is a good-sized plum. Here is the full transcript to an oval office interview between Trump and CBS reporter John Dickerson on May 1, 2017.

The context to this interview is Trump's false accusation that the Obama administration had tapped his phone. Trump took to Twitter and labeled former President Barack Obama as being "sick and bad." It is a perfect example of Trump deceit and no Trump library would be complete without it:

**JOHN DICKERSON:** Did President Obama give you any advice that was helpful? That you think, wow, he really was—

**DONALD TRUMP:** --Well, he was very nice to me. But after that, we've had some difficulties. So, it doesn't matter. You know, words are less important to me than deeds. And you—you saw what happened with surveillance. And everybody saw what happened with surveillance—

**JOHN DICKERSON:** Difficulties how?

**DONALD TRUMP:** --and I thought that—well, you saw what happened with surveillance. And I think that was inappropriate, but that's the way—

**JOHN DICKERSON:** What does that mean, sir?

**DONALD TRUMP:** You can figure that out yourself.

**JOHN DICKERSON:** Well, I—the reason I ask is you said he was—you called him "sick and bad."

**DONALD TRUMP:** Look, you can figure it out yourself. He was very nice to me with words, but—and when I was with him—but after that, there has been no relationship.

**JOHN DICKERSON:** But you stand by that claim about him?

**DONALD TRUMP:** I don't stand by anything. I just—you can take it the way you want. I think our side's been proven very strongly. And everybody's talking about it. And frankly it should be discussed. I think that is a very big surveillance of our citizens. I think it's a very big topic. And it's a topic that should be number one. And we should find out what the hell is going on.

**JOHN DICKERSON:** I just wanted to find out, though. You're—you're the president of the United States. You said he was "sick and bad" because he had tapped you—I'm just—

**DONALD TRUMP:** You can take—any way. You can take it any way you want.

**JOHN DICKERSON:** But I'm asking you. Because you don't want to be—

**DONALD TRUMP:** You don't—

**JOHN DICKERSON:** --fake news. I want to hear it from—

**DONALD TRUMP:** You don't have to—

**JOHN DICKERSON:** --President Trump.

**DONALD TRUMP:** --ask me. You don't have to ask me.

**JOHN DICKERSON:** Why not?

**DONALD TRUMP:** Because I have my own opinions. You can have your own opinions.

**JOHN DIKERSON:** But I want to know your opinions. You're the president of the United States.

**DONALD TRUMP:** Okay, it's enough. Thank you. Thank you very much.

# Trump-Putin meeting

You will agree that the story of Trump is one that can always use a few more words. In Chapter 31 of this novel, Leslie talks about that fateful, and highly suspicious, meeting between Trump and Putin. It was on Monday, July 16, 2018 that those two snuck away for a couple of hours and had a good secret chat. No one knows what was said in that meeting since the translator dictation was destroyed. But we do have a transcript of the press conference that followed the meeting. This is presented by Jennie Neufeld of Vox:

President Donald Trump met with Russian President Vladimir Putin on Monday to discuss relations between the two countries. The press conference that followed was striking. Asked to denounce Russian interference in the 2016 election, Trump changed the subject to Hillary Clinton's emails. Trump refused, despite being asked multiple times, to criticize Putin, blamed the US for tensions with Russia, and repeatedly criticized the investigation into whether his campaign colluded with Russia in 2016.

A rush transcript of the press conference follows.

---

**VLADIMIR PUTIN:** Thank you so much. Shall we start working, I guess?

Distinguished Mr. President, ladies and gentlemen, negotiations with the President of the United States, Donald Trump, took place in a frank and business-like atmosphere. I think we can call it a success and a very fruitful round of negotiations. We carefully analyzed the current status, the present and the future of the Russia-United States relationship — key issues of the global agenda.

It's quite clear to everyone that the bilateral relationship are going through a complicated stage. Yet those impediments, the current tension, the tense atmosphere essentially have no solid reason behind it. The Cold War is a thing of past. The era of acute ideological confrontation of the two countries is a thing of the remote past — it's a vestige of the past. The situation of the world changed dramatically. Today both Russia and the United States face a whole new set of challenges. Those include a dangerous maladjustment of mechanisms for maintaining international security and stability, regional crises, the creeping threat of terrorism and transnational crime. It's the snowballing problems in the economy, environmental risks and other sets of challenges. We can only cope with these challenges if we join the ranks and work together. Hopefully, we will reach this understanding with our American partners.

Today's negotiations reflected our joint wish, our joint wish with President Trump, to redress this negative situation in the bilateral relationship, outline first steps for improving this relationship to restore the acceptable level of trust, and going back to the previous level of interaction on all mutual interests and issues.

As major nuclear powers, we bear special responsibility for maintaining international security. It's vital — and we mentioned this during the negotiations — it's crucial that we fine-tune the dialogue on strategic stability and global security and nonproliferation on weapons of mass destruction. We submitted to our American colleagues a note with a number of specific suggestions. We believe it necessary to work together further to interact on the disarmament agenda, military and technical cooperation. This includes the extension of the Strategic Offensive Arms Limitation Treaty. It's a dangerous situation with the global American anti-missile defense system. It's the implementation issue with the INF Treaty. And of course the agenda of non-placement of weapons in space.

We favor the continued cooperation in counterterrorism and maintaining cybersecurity. I'd like to point out specifically that our special services are cooperating quite successfully together. The most recent example is their operational cooperation within the recently concluded World football Cup. In general, the contacts among our special services should be put to system-wide basis, should be brought to a systemic framework. I reminded President Trump about the suggestion to re-establish the working group on anti-terrorism. We mentioned a plethora of regional crises, not always that our postures dovetail exactly, and yet the overlapping and mutual interests abound. We have to look for points of contact and interact closer in a variety of international forums.

Clearly, we mentioned the regional crisis, for instance, Syria. As far as Syria is concerned, the task of establishing peace and reconciliation in this country could be the first showcase example of the successful joint work. Russia and the United States apparently can proactively take leadership on this issue and organize the interaction to overcome humanitarian crisis and help Syrian refugees go back to their homes. In order to accomplish this level of successful cooperation in Syria, we have all the required components. Let me remind you that both Russian and American military have acquired a useful experience of coordination of their action, established the operational channels of communication, which permitted [us] to avoid dangerous incidents and unintentional collisions in the air and on the ground. Also, crushing terrorists in the southwest of Syria: The south of Syria should be brought to the full compliance with the treaty of 1974 about the separation of forces, about separation of forces of Israel and Syria. This will bring peace to Golan Heights. And bring more peaceful relationship between Syria and Israel and also to provide security of the state of Israel. Mr. President paid special attention to the issue during today's negotiations. I would like to confirm that Russia is interested in this development and this will act accordingly. Thus far, we will make a step toward creating a lasting peace in compliance with the respective resolutions of security council, for instance the resolution 338.

We're glad that the Korean peninsula issue is starting to resolve. To a great extent, it was possible thanks to the personal engagement of President Trump who opted for dialogue instead of confrontation.

We also mentioned our concern about the withdrawal of the United States from the JCPOA. Well, the US — our US counterparts are aware of our posture. Let me remind you that thanks to the Iranian nuclear deal, Iran became most controlled country in the world. It submitted to the control of IAEA. It effectively ensures the exclusively peaceful nature of Iranian nuclear program and strengthens the non-proliferation regime.

While we discussed the internal Ukrainian crisis, we paid special attention to the bonafide implementation of Minsk agreements by Kiev. At the same time, the United States could be more decisive in nudging the Ukrainian leadership and encourage it to work actively on this.

We paid more attention to economic ties and economic cooperation. It's clear that both countries, the businesses of both countries are interested in this. The American delegation was one of the largest delegations in the St. Petersburg economic forum. It featured over 500 representatives from American businesses. We agreed, me and President Trump, we agreed to create a high-level working group that would bring together captains of Russian and American business. After all, entrepreneurs and businessmen know better how to articulate this successful business cooperation. We'll let them think and make their proposals and suggestions in this regard.

Once again, President Trump mentioned the issue of the so-called interference of Russia in the American elections. I had to reiterate things I said several times, including during our personal contacts, that the Russian state has never interfered and is not going to interfere into internal American affairs, including the election process. Any specific material, if such things arise, we are ready to analyze together. For instance, we can analyze them through the joint working group on cyber security, the establishment of which we discussed during our previous contacts.

Clearly, it's past time we restore our cooperation in the cultural area in the humanitarian area. As far as that, I think you know that recently we hosted the American congressmen delegation. Now it's portrayed almost as a historic event, although it should have been just a current affair, just business as usual. In this regard, we mentioned this proposal to the president. We have to think about practicalities of our cooperation, but also about the rationality, the logic of it. We have to engage experts on bilateral relationship who know history and the background of our relationship. The idea is to create an expert council that would include political scientists, prominent diplomats and former military experts in both countries who would look for points of contact between the two countries. That would look for ways of putting the relationship on the trajectory of growth.

In general, we are glad with the outcome of our first full-scale meeting because previously we only had a chance to talk briefly on international forums. We had good conversation with President Trump. I hope that we start to understand each other better. I'm grateful to Donald for it. Clearly, there are some challenges left — we were not able to clear all the backlog. But I think that we made the first important step in this direction. In conclusion, I want to point out that this atmosphere of cooperation is something that we are especially grateful for to our Finnish hosts. We're grateful for Finnish people and Finnish leadership for what they have done. I know that we have caused some inconvenience to Finland and we apologize for it. Thank you for your attention.

**DONALD TRUMP:** Thank you very much. Thank you. I have just concluded a meeting with President Putin on a wide range of critical issues for both of our countries. We had direct, open, deeply productive dialogue. It went very well. Before I begin, I want to thank President Niinistö of Finland for graciously hosting today's summit. President Putin and I were saying how lovely it was and what a great job they did. I also want to congratulate Russia and President Putin for having done such an excellent job in hosting the World Cup. It was really one of the best ever. Your team also did very well. It was a great job.

I'm here today to continue the proud tradition of bold American diplomacy. From the earliest days of our republic, American leaders have to understand that diplomacy and engagement is preferable to conflict and hostility. A productive dialogue is not only good for the United States and good for Russia, but it is good for the world.

The disagreements between our two countries are well-known. President Putin and I discussed them at length today. But if we're going to solve many of the problems facing our world, then we're going to have to find ways to cooperate in pursuit of shared interests.

Too often, in both recent past and long ago, we have seen the consequences when diplomacy is left on the table. We have also seen the benefits of cooperation. In the last century, our nations fought alongside one another in the second World War. Even during the tensions of the Cold War, when the world looked much different than it does today, the United States and Russia were able to maintain a strong dialogue. Our relationship has never been worse than it is now. However, that changed as of about four hours ago. I really believe that. Nothing would be easier politically than to refuse to meet, to refuse to engage. But that would not accomplish anything.

As president, I cannot make decisions on foreign policy in a futile effort to appease partisan critics or the media or Democrats who want to do nothing but resist and obstruct. Constructive dialogue between the United States and Russia forwards the opportunity to open new pathways toward peace and stability in our world. I would rather take a political risk in pursuit of peace than to risk peace in pursuit of politics. As president, I will always put what is best for America and what is best for the American people.

During today's meeting, I addressed directly with President Putin the issue of Russian interference in our elections. I felt this was a message best delivered in person. Spent a great deal of time talking about it. President Putin may very well want to address it and very strongly, because he feels very strongly about it. And he has an interesting idea.

We also discussed one of the most critical challenges facing humanity, nuclear proliferation. I provided an update on my meeting last month with Chairman Kim on the denuclearization of North Korea. After today, I am very sure that President Putin and Russia want very much to end that problem. Going to work with us. I appreciate that commitment.

The president and I also discussed the scourge of radical Islamic terrorism. Both Russia and the United States have suffered horrific terrorist attacks. We have agreed to maintain open communication between our security agencies to protect our citizens from this global menace. Last year, we told Russia about a planned attack in St.

Petersburg and they were able to stop it cold. They found them. They stopped them. There was no doubt about it. I appreciated President Putin's phone call afterwards to thank me.

I also emphasized the importance of placing pressure on Iran to halt its nuclear ambitions and to stop its campaign of violence throughout the area, throughout the Middle East. As we discussed at length, the crisis in Syria is a complex one. Cooperation between our two countries has the potential to save hundreds of thousands of lives. I also made clear that the United States will not allow Iran to benefit from our successful campaign against ISIS. We have just about eradicated ISIS in the area. We also agreed that representatives from our national security councils will meet to follow-up on all of the issues we addressed today and to continue the progress we have started right here in Helsinki.

Today's meeting is only the beginning of a longer process. But we have taken the first steps toward a brighter future and one with a strong dialogue and a lot of thought. Our expectations are grounded in realism, but our hopes are grounded in Americans' desire for friendship, cooperation, and peace. I think I can speak on behalf of Russia when I say that also. President Putin, I want to thank you again for joining me for these important discussions and for advancing open dialogue between Russia and the United States. Our meeting carries on a long tradition of diplomacy between Russia, the United States for the greater good of all. This was a very constructive day. This was a very constructive few hours that we spent together. It's in the interest of both of our countries to continue our conversation. And we have agreed to do so. I'm sure we will be meeting again in the future often, and hopefully, we will solve every one of the problems that we discussed today. Again, President Putin, thank you very much.

**REPORTER:** (Alexei Meshkov from Interfax Information Agency): Good afternoon. I have a question to President trump. During your recent European tour, you mentioned that theimplementation of the Nord Stream 2 gas pipeline makes Europe [a] hostage of Russia. You suggested that you could free Europe from this by supplying American LNG (liquefied natural gas). This cold winter showed the current model, current mechanism of supply of fuel to Europe is quite viable. At the same time, as far as I know, the US had to buy Russian gas for Boston.

I have a question. The implementation of your idea has political tinge to it or is this practical one? Because there will be a gap formed in the supply and demand mechanism and first it's the consuming countries who will fall into this gap.

The second question, before the meeting with President Putin, you called him an adversary, a rival. And yet you expressed hope [that] you will be able to bring this relationship to a new level. Did you manage to do this?

**TRUMP:** I called him a competitor and a good competitor he is. I think the word competitor is a compliment. I think that we will be competing when you talk about the pipeline. I'm not sure necessarily that it's in the best interests of Germany or not. That was a decision that they made. We will be competing. As you know, the United States is now, or soon will be, but I think it is right now the largest in the oil and gas world. So we're going to be selling LNG. We'll have to be competing with the pipeline. I think we will compete successfully. Although there is a little advantage locationally. I wish them luck. I discussed with Angela Merkel in pretty strong tones. But, I also know where they're coming from. They have a very close source. We will see how that all works out. But we have lots of sources now. The United States is much different than it was a number of years ago when we weren't able to extract what we can extract today. So, today, we're number one in the world at that. I think we will be out there competing very strongly. Thank you very much.

**PUTIN:** If I may, I throw in some two cents. We talked to Mr. President, including this subject as well. We are aware of the stance of President Trump. I think that we as major oil and gas power and I think the United States is a major gas and oil power as well. We can work together on regulation of international markets because neither of us is actually interested in the plummeting of the prices. And the consumers will suffer as well. And the consumers in the United States will suffer as well. And the shale gas production will suffer. Because beyond a certain price bracket, it's no longer profitable to produce gas. Nor we are interested in driving prices up, because it will drain live juices from all other sectors of the economy. We do have space for cooperation here, as the first thing.

Then about the North Stream, Mr. President voiced his concerns about the possibility of disappearance of transit through Ukraine. I reassured Mr. President that Russia stands ready to maintain this transit. Moreover, we stand ready to extend this transit contract that's about to expire next year in case. If the dispute between the economic entities — dispute will be settled in Stockholm arbitration court.

**REPORTER:** (Jeff Mason from Reuters): Thank you. Mr. President, you tweeted this morning that it's US Foolishness, stupidity and the Mueller probe that is responsible for the decline in US Relations with Russia. Do you hold Russia at all accountable for anything in particular? If so, what would you consider them that they are responsible for?

**TRUMP:** Yes, I do. I hold both countries responsibility. I think the United States has been foolish. I think we have all been foolish. We should have had this dialogue a long time ago, a long time frankly before I got to office. I think we're all to blame. I think that the United States now has stepped forward along with Russia. We're getting together and we have a chance to do some great things, whether it's nuclear proliferation in terms of stopping, we have to do it — ultimately, that's probably the most important thing that we can be working on.

I do feel that we have both made some mistakes. I think that the probe is a disaster for our country. I think it's kept us apart. It's kept us separated. There was no collusion at all. Everybody knows it. People are being brought out to the fore. So far that I know, virtually, none of it related to the campaign. They will have to try really hard to find something that did relate to the campaign. That was a clean campaign. I beat Hillary Clinton easily and, frankly, we beat her. And I'm not even saying from the standpoint — we won that race. It's a shame there could be a cloud over it. People know that. People understand it. The main thing — and we discussed this also — is zero collusion. It has had a negative impact upon the relationship of the two largest nuclear powers in the world. We have 90 percent of nuclear power between the two countries. It's ridiculous. It's ridiculous what's going on with the probe.

**REPORTER:** (Jeff Mason from Reuters): For President Putin if I could follow up as well. Why should Americans and why should President Trump believe your statement that Russia did not intervene in the 2016 election given the evidence that US Intelligence agencies have provided? Will you consider extraditing the 12 Russian officials that were indicted last week by a US Grand jury.

**TRUMP:** Well I'm going to let the president answer the second part of that question.

As you know, the concept of that came up perhaps a little before, but it came out as a reason why the Democrats lost an election, which frankly, they should have been able to win, because the electoral college is much more advantageous for Democrats, as you know, than it is to Republicans. We won the electoral college by a lot. 306 to 223, I believe. That was a well-fought battle. We did a great job.

Frankly, I'm going to let the president speak to the second part of your question. But, just to say it one time again and I say it all the time, there was no collusion. I didn't know the president. There was nobody to colluded with. There was no collusion with the campaign. Every time you hear all of these 12 and 14 — it's stuff that has nothing to do — and frankly, they admit, these are not people involved in the campaign. But to the average reader out there, they are saying, well maybe that does. It doesn't. Even the people involved, some perhaps told mis-stories. In one case the FBI said there was no lie. There was no lie. Somebody else said there was. We ran a brilliant campaign. And that's why I'm president. Thank you.

**PUTIN:** As to who is to be believed, who is not to be believed: you can trust no one. Where did you get this idea that President Trump trusts me or I trust him? He defends the interests of the United States of America and I do defend the interests of the Russian Federation. We do have interests that are common. We are looking for points of contact.

There are issues where our postures diverge and we are looking for ways to reconcile our differences, how to make our effort more meaningful. We should not proceed from the immediate political interests that guide certain political powers in our countries. We should be guided by facts. Could you name a single fact that would definitively prove the collusion? This is utter nonsense — just like the president recently mentioned. Yes, the public at large in the United States had a certain perceived opinion of the candidates during the campaign. But there's nothing particularly extraordinary about it. That's usual thing.

President Trump, when he was a candidate, he mentioned the need to restore the Russia/US relationship and it's clear that certain parts of American society felt sympathetic about it and different people could express their sympathy in different ways. Isn't that natural? Isn't it natural to be sympathetic towards a person who is willing to restore the relationship with our country, who wants to work with us?

We heard the accusations about it. As far as I know, this company hired American lawyers and the accusations doesn't have a fighting chance in the American courts. There's no evidence when it comes to the actual facts. So we have to be guided by facts, not by rumors.

Now, let's get back to the issue of this 12 alleged intelligence officers of Russia. I don't know the full extent of the situation. But President Trump mentioned this issue. I will look into it.

So far, I can say the following. Things that are off the top of my head. We have an existing agreement between the United States of America and the Russian Federation, an existing treaty that dates back to 1999. The mutual assistance on criminal cases. This treaty is in full effect. It works quite efficiently. On average, we initiate about 100, 150 criminal cases upon request from foreign states.

For instance, the last year, there was one extradition case upon the request sent by the United States. This treaty has specific legal procedures we can offer. The appropriate commission headed by

Special Attorney Mueller, he can use this treaty as a solid foundation and send a formal, official request to us so that we could interrogate, hold questioning of these individuals who he believes are privy to some crimes. Our enforcement are perfectly able to do this questioning and send the appropriate materials to the United States. Moreover, we can meet you halfway. We can make another step. We can actually permit representatives of the United States, including the members of this very commission headed by Mr. Mueller, we can let them into the country. They can be present at questioning.

In this case, there's another condition. This kind of effort should be mutual one. Then we would expect that the Americans would reciprocate. They would question officials, including the officers of law enforcement and intelligence services of the United States whom we believe have something to do with illegal actions on the territory of Russia. And we have to request the presence of our law enforcement.

For instance, we can bring up Mr. Browder in this particular case. Business associates of Mr. Browder have earned over $1.5 billion in Russia. They never paid any taxes. Neither in Russia nor in the United States. Yet, the money escapes the country. They were transferred to the United States. They sent huge amount of money, $400 million as a contribution to the campaign of Hillary Clinton. Well, that's their personal case. It might have been legal, the contribution itself. But the way the money was earned was illegal. We have solid reason to believe that some intelligence officers, guided these transactions. So we have an interest of questioning them. That could be a first step. We can extend also it. Options abound. They all can be found in an appropriate legal framework.

**REPORTER:** (Jeff Mason from Reuters): President Putin, did you want President Trump to win the election and did you direct any of your officials to help him do that?

**PUTIN:** Yes, I did. Yes, I did. Because he talked about bringing the US/Russia relationship back to normal.

**REPORTER:** (Ilya Petrenko from RT International): Mr. President, would you please go into the details of possibly any specific arrangements for the US to work together with Russia in Syria — if any of these arrangements were made today or discussed?

My question to President Putin in Russian. Since we brought up the issue of football, several times, I use the football language. Mr. Pompeo mentioned that when we talk about Syrian cooperation, the ball is in the Syrian court. Mr. Putin, in Russian court, is it true? How would you use this fact of having the ball?

**TRUMP:** Well, I guess I will answer the first part of the question. We have worked with Israel long and hard for many years, many decades. I think we have never, never has any country been closer than we are.

President Putin also is helping Israel. We both spoke with Bibi Netanyahu. They would like to do certain things with respect to Syria, having to do with the safety of Israel. In that respect, we absolutely would like to work in order to help Israel. Israel will be working with us. So both countries would work jointly. I think that when you look at all of the progress that's been made in certain sections with the eradication of ISIS, about 98 percent, 99 percent there, and other things that have taken place that we have done and that, frankly, Russia has helped us with in certain respects. But I think that working with Israel is a great thing. And creating safety for Israel is something that both President Putin and I would like to see very much.

One little thing I might add to that is the helping of people. Helping of people. Because you have such horrible. I've seen reports and I've seen pictures. I've seen just about everything. If we can do something to help the people of Syria get back into some form of shelter and on a humanitarian basis. That's what the word was, a humanitarian basis. I think both of us would be very interested in doing that. And we are. And we will do that. Thank you very much.

**REPORTER:** (Ilya Petrenko from RT International): For now, no specific agreements, for instance, between the militaries?

**TRUMP:** Well, our militaries do get along. Our militaries have gotten along probably better than our political leaders for years. Our militaries do get along very well. They do coordinate in Syria and other places. Okay? Thank you.

**PUTIN:** Yes, we did mention this. We mentioned the humanitarian trek of this issue. Yesterday, I discussed this with French president, Mr. Macron. And we reached an agreement that together with European countries, including France, we will step up this effort. On our behalf, we will provide military cargo aircraft to deliver humanitarian cargo. Today, I brought up this issue with President Trump. I think there's plenty of things to look into.

The crucial thing is that huge amount of refugees are in Turkey, in Lebanon, in Jordan, in the states that border or adjacent to Syria. If we help them, the migratory pressure upon the European states will be decreased many fold. I believe it's crucial from any point of view from humanitarian point of view, from the point of view of helping people, helping the refugees. And in general, I agree, I concur with President Trump, our military cooperate quite successfully together. They do get along and I hope they will be able to do so in [the] future. We will keep working in Russia, Turkey and Iran, which I informed President Trump.

But we do stand ready to link this effort to the so-called small group of states so that the process would be a broader one, it would be a multidimensional one. We will be able to maximize our fighting chance to gather ultimate success on the issue of Syria.

Speaking about having the ball in our court in Syria. President Trump has just mentioned that we have successfully concluded the world football cup. Speaking of the football, actually, Mr. President, I will give this ball to you and now the ball is in your court. [Applause] All the more that the United States will host the world cup in 2026.

**TRUMP:** That's right. Thank you very much. We do host it. We hope we do as good a job. That's very nice. That will go to my son, Barron. We have no question. Melania, here you go.

**REPORTER:** (Jonathan Lemire from AP): Thank you. A question for each president. President Trump, you first. Just now President Putin denied having anything to do with the election interference in 2016. Every US intelligence agency has concluded that Russia did.

My first question for you, sir, is who do you believe? My second question is would you now with the whole world watching tell President Putin — would you denounce what happened in 2016 and would you warn him to never do it again?

**TRUMP:** So let me just say that we have two thoughts. You have groups that are wondering why the FBI never took the server. Why haven't they taken the server? Why was the FBI told to leave the office of the democratic national committee? I've been wondering that. I've been asking that for months and months and I've been tweeting it out and calling it out on social media. Where is the server? I want to know, where is the server and what is the server saying? With that being said, all I can do is ask the question. My people came to me, Dan Coats came to me and some others and said they think it's Russia.

I have President Putin. He just said it's not Russia. I will say this. I don't see any reason why it would be, but I really do want to see the server. But I have confidence in both parties. I really believe that this will probably go on for a while, but I don't think it can go on without finding out what happened to the server. What happened to the servers of the Pakistani gentleman that worked on the DNC? Where are those servers? They're missing. Where are they? What happened to Hillary Clinton's emails? 33,000 emails gone — just gone. I think in Russia they wouldn't be gone so easily. I think it's a disgrace that we can't get Hillary Clinton's 33,000 emails. So I have great confidence in my intelligence people, but I will tell you that president Putin was extremely strong and powerful in his denial today. And what he did is an incredible offer. He offered to have the people working on the case come and work with their investigators, with respect to the 12 people. I think that's an incredible offer. Okay thank you.

**PUTIN:** I'd like to add something to this. After all, I was an intelligence officer myself. And I do know how dossiers are made up. Just a second. That's the first thing. Not the second thing. I believe that Russia is a democratic state and I hope you're not denying this right to your own country, you're not denying that United States is democracy. Do you believe the United States is a democracy? And if so, if it is a democratic state, then the final conclusion in this kind of dispute can only be delivered by a trial, by the court. Not by the executive, by the law enforcement.

For instance, the concord company that is brought up is being accused, it's being accused of interference, but this company does not constitute the Russian state. It does not represent the Russian state. And I brought several examples before.

Well, you have a lot of individuals in the United States — take George Soros, for instance, with multibillion capitals, but it doesn't make him — his position, his posture the posture of the United States. No, it does not. It's the same case. There is the issue of trying a case in the court and the final say is for the court to deliver.

We are now talking about the individuals and not about particular states. And as far as the most recent allegations is concerned about the Russian intelligence officers, we do have an intergovernmental treaty. Please do send us the request. We will analyze it properly and we'll send a formal response. As I said, we can extend this cooperation, but we should do it on a reciprocal basis. Because we would await our Russian counterparts to provide us access to the persons of interests for us who we believe can have something to do with intelligence service.

Let's discuss the specific issues and not use the Russia and US Relationship as a loose change for this internal political struggle.

**REPORTER:** (Jonathan Lemire from AP): A question for President Putin, thank you. Two questions for you, sir. Can you tell me what President Trump may have indicated to you about officially recognizing Crimea as part of Russia? And secondly, sir, do you --

does the Russian government have any compromising material on President Trump or his family?

**PUTIN:** President Trump — well, the posture of President Trump on Crimea is well known and he stands firmly by it. He continues to maintain that it was illegal to annex it. Our viewpoint is different. We held a referendum in strict compliance with the UN Charter and international legislation. For us this issue --we put [unintelligible] to this issue.

And now to the compromising material. Yeah, I did hear these rumors that we allegedly collected compromising material on Mr. Trump when he was visiting Moscow. Well, distinguished colleague, let me tell you this, when President Trump was in Moscow back then, I didn't even know that he was in Moscow. I treat President Trump with utmost respect, but back then when he was a private individual, a businessman, nobody informed me that he was in Moscow.

Let's take St. Petersburg economic forum, for instance. There were over 500 American businessmen — high-ranking, high-level ones. I don't even remember the last names of each and every one. Do you think that we try to collect compromising material on each and every single one of them?

Well, it's difficult to imagine utter nonsense on a bigger scale than this. Please disregard these issues and don't think about this anymore again.

**TRUMP:** And I have to say if they had it, it would have been out long ago. And if anybody watched Peter Strzok testify over the last couple of days, and I was in Brussels watching it, it was a disgrace to the FBI. It was a disgrace to our country. And you would say, 'That was a total witch hunt.' Thank you very much, everybody.

# KRAZY KAT 2020, a Misadventure in the Age of Trump

## 1

**3**

**4**

**5**

**6**

**7**

**8**

187

**11**

I've heard say it could be impeached.

BECAUSE
YOU'RE THE
OTHER!

# 20

# ABOUT THE AUTHOR

Henry Chamberlain is an artist and writer. Henry enjoys visual and literary art equally and seeks to combine both passions whenever possible as he does in his work in comics, graphic novels and prose with illustrations. You can find him at comicsgrinder.com as well as henrychamberlain.com.

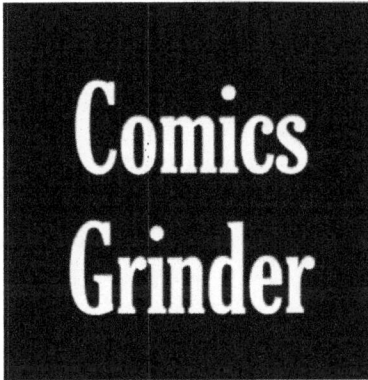

This is a Comics Grinder Production.
Comicsgrinder.com

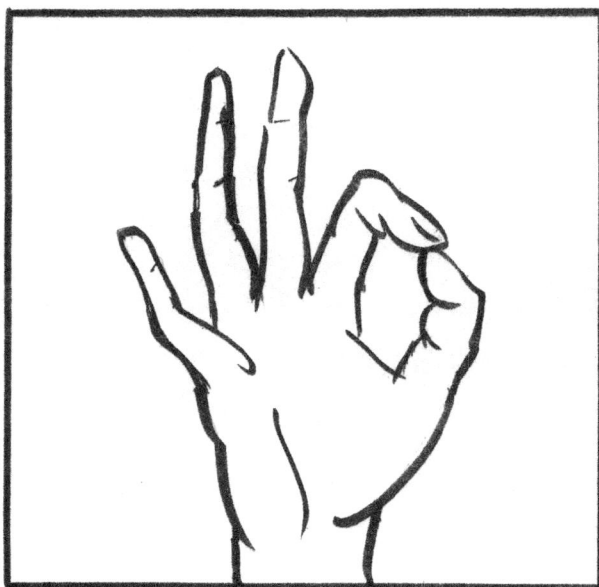

Made in the USA
Las Vegas, NV
28 February 2022